Spell of the Seven Stones

by

JANE DONNELLY

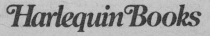

Harlequin Books

TORONTO • LONDON • NEW YORK • AMSTERDAM
SYDNEY • HAMBURG • PARIS

Original hardcover edition published in 1978
by Mills & Boon Limited

ISBN 0-373-02217-4

Harlequin edition published December 1978

PRINTED IN U.S.A

Sophy quivered with shock and frustration

She just couldn't say what she wanted to Robert's face. Imagine him giving orders in her house! To release her pent-up fury, she went into her workroom, got out some clay, and began to pummel it with violent energy.

She wasn't modeling so much as shoving a head together and gouging out features; but it wasn't a bad likeness of Robert Carlton. His friends might not recognize him, but his enemies would.

When she'd finished, Sophy stood back and said, "Hello and goodbye," then bashed his head back into a lump of clay.

If only she could rid herself of that man as easily!

OTHER
Harlequin Romances
by JANE DONNELLY

Many of these titles are available at your local bookseller
or through the Harlequin Reader Service.

For a free catalogue listing all available Harlequin Romances,
send your name and address to:

HARLEQUIN READER SERVICE,
M.P.O. Box 707, Niagara Falls, N.Y. 14302
Canadian address: Stratford, Ontario, Canada N5A 6W2

or use coupon at back of book.

CHAPTER ONE

SOPHY BROWN came to Halebridge at dusk. She wished she had arrived earlier, when the sun was shining. That was how she had seen this village on the edge of the Yorkshire dales five weeks ago, when she had been lured here by the advertisement 'Pottery workroom and shop for sale, cottage living accommodation.'

She had been sitting by the river Thames at Richmond, feeding the ducks with her sandwiches, and leafing through a property magazine. There were several crafts shops going, but this was the only one that offered a pottery and she had put a cross by it.

As soon as she got back to work she would phone and fix an appointment. She had some time-off owing and she was going to use it to find somewhere in which she could invest her small legacy from her father and her own talents and energy.

Not that she wasn't happy in her work where she was. She was a professional potter, making the products and helping to sell them, and she liked the women she worked for. She liked her roomy bedsitter, just off Richmond Hill, and the man who said he loved her. But she had to get right away and waste no time in doing it.

So after five harassing weeks she was arriving with two large suitcases of clothes, to spend her first night in her new home sleeping on a camp bed; and tomorrow the removal van would bring the rest of her belongings.

Everywhere had looked sparkling and bright in the

sunshine, but now the houses were grey and the streets were quiet. The Potter's Wheel, which was the name of her property, was in a cobbled side lane, backed by a small tangled garden with a hill behind it. Not a particularly high hill, compared with some round here, rising to a plateau and topped by a cluster of tall rugged standing stones.

She had been fascinated by them when she saw them. There was nothing like a bit of prehistory to give a feeling of peace and security. They were known as the Seven Brothers, she had been told, and she liked the sound of that too. Seven strong friendly men watching over her, and causing no trouble because they couldn't take a step or say a word.

But now, in the half light, the stones looked sinister against the skyline and the trees were very dark. There was a little wood up there. She wondered if the stones ever moved into the wood. If she might look out of her bathroom window at—three o'clock in the morning, say, the hour of the wolf—and see the patch where the Seven Brothers stood quite bare and empty.

She jumped quickly out of her car, and the shop door was opened by a girl who said, 'Hello, I was beginning to wonder if you'd lost your way,' as though she was glad to see her.

'Sorry,' said Sophy, 'I didn't get away as early as I'd planned.'

There had been a final thunderous row with Stewart and she had driven slower because of it. It had left her so shaking that she had been undecided whether to postpone the drive from London to Yorkshire until tomorrow. But she had to be here when her furniture and packing cases arrived, and she had handed over the key of her empty bedsitter, and if she'd asked a friend to put her up Stewart might have carried on the row all night.

He was sincere in his anger and resentment, but he was an actor and he relished scenes of high drama. His parting cry had been, 'How can you do this? We've been so good together, how can you throw it all away?'

It had sounded like a quote from a bad play, and she had wondered how he would have reacted if she'd said, 'Because you're reminding me of my father, and he was a born jailer.'

She was in the car by then. 'Goodbye,' she'd called, 'I'll write, I'll phone,' and she'd edged her estate car into the moving stream of traffic. But it was a good hour later before she could trust herself to relax a little.

'Sorry,' she said again now. 'I hope I haven't kept you hanging about, although it's lovely to be welcomed.'

The girl was dressed for a date, and not with another girl who had just moved into an empty house. Her name was Jenine Riggs, and she had been helping at the Potter's Wheel ever since she left school. She was twenty now, a year younger than Sophy, willowy, with smooth fair hair falling from a centre parting.

She was staying on in the business, for a while at least. Partly because Sophy obviously couldn't be in the workroom and the shop at the same time; and partly because Sophy had liked her when they'd met, and felt that it would be good to have a friend around when she started on her lonely venture.

Jenine had a fire burning in the living room of the house, and food in the kitchen to tide Sophy over the next few days. The gas stove was a fixture, and Jenine explained, 'There's bread and butter and bacon and eggs, and some tinned stuff.'

'That's very kind of you. Thank you very much.' The fire and the food had been arranged and promised, but it was nice of Jenine to stay and welcome Sophy, especially as she was wearing a flowing floral dress, with a three-tiered skirt, and a black velvet jacket slung over her shoulders.

'I'll be off, then,' she said.

'Got a date?' Of course she had a date. Her eyes brightened and her smile was radiant.

'Yes, but it's all right, he'll wait for me.'

Sophy envied her her certainty, and as she heard the sound of Jenine's footsteps over the cobblestones, light and quick because she was running, she heard herself give a deep sigh.

This was no way to start. She had chosen to come here. She need not have been lonely tonight, or any night. She could still have been in her cosy bedsitter, with friends to talk to and laugh with; instead of standing alone in an almost empty shop, with no sound at all, not even the footsteps now.

It did look rather bleak. Blinds were drawn at the windows, and there were gaps between the goods on the shelves. She had taken on some of the stock from the previous owners, who had made attractive serviceable domestic ware, and some of her own work would be arriving tomorrow in the furniture van. Then she and Jenine would set about arranging the shelves, and she would start in the workroom.

She was looking forward to getting her hands into clay, creating again. It was a satisfying way of earning a living, and she was fortunate to be able to buy her own small pottery.

This place was hers, all her own, and that was what she was struggling for, a place to call her own, a life to call her own.

She put her car in the garage and brought in her suitcases. There wasn't much point in carrying them upstairs until tomorrow. Until tomorrow there would be nothing else upstairs and then one of the two bedrooms would be furnished. So she left them in the living room in which, apart from a telephone on the floor, there was a small table and a chair, and a camp bed complete with sleeping bag, all of which had been borrowed from Jenine.

Then she made herself a strong cup of coffee and a plate of corned beef sandwiches, then sat in front of the fire, and decided to get a cat or a dog, because she had never really lived alone before and empty rooms might get on top of her after a while.

Her bedsitter had been in a house full of bedsitters, and before that she had lived in her father's home. It was a house in a town, she wasn't used to this depth of silence.

She was going to miss her friends. She wanted to phone them now and say she was here and safe, and tomorrow when her furniture was around her she would. Familiar voices, at the moment, might make her feel even more alone.

But it was going to be comfortable when she had her things: the bright rugs, and the furniture she had spotted in junk shops and auctions over the past two years, and taken home in triumph, piece by piece. She had an instinctive feel for design that made her art teacher at school talk about her going to art college after A-levels.

But her father was having none of that. He distrusted students, especially the crowd from the local further education college. Few of them, in his opinion, did much studying, but they could be relied on to cause aggravation and confusion at every opportunity.

He wanted his daughter keeping well clear of them, and Sophy had always accepted that his word was law.

In every material way he had been a good father. She couldn't remember her mother and it couldn't have been easy for him, left with a daughter only two years old. He was a man's man, a highly respected Chief Inspector, and a succession of women looked after the house, and helped to care for Sophy. But none of them was on first-name terms with her employer. There was never any familiarity at all.

It didn't seem odd to Sophy that he never married again. He was quite distinguished-looking, a tall lean man who rarely smiled, but she couldn't imagine him loving anyone. Caring for them, doing his duty by them, yes; but his work was always his first love, and his leisure companions were always men, often his colleagues. He played golf and chess. He was a member of Rotary and the local Conservative Club, and she knew how highly he was esteemed, by the letters she received when he died.

She was sure he had all the virtues they were telling her about. An honourable, courageous man, a scholar and a gentleman. But in all the years she had lived with him she had never once felt close to him. When she hurt herself as a child she ran to whoever was looking after her. When she was older she brought her problems home from school to the woman in the kitchen. They stayed quite a while, there had been four in nineteen years, because the wages were fair and the house wasn't hard to run, and they had all become fond of Sophy.

When she wanted to go to art school Mrs Benson, the last of the four, had been their housekeeper. She lived with her own family and came in each day, and had the highest esteem for the Inspector. She thought that Sophy's paintings and models were very good. Sometimes she took one home with her. She had a couple of flower prints framed on her sitting room wall, and a baked clay cat Sophy made her for a birthday present, on the mantelshelf.

But Mrs Benson wasn't surprised when the Inspector put his foot down. 'Wouldn't hear of it,' she told her husband that night. 'Sophy's got to take a secretary's course first, and she can go on doing her paintings, but she isn't going to no art school.'

Mr Benson's sympathies were with the Inspector. 'Well, you know what these students get up to,' he said sagely. 'He's got a well brought up girl there. She's a credit to him. He doesn't want her getting into any trouble.'

'A private commercial college,' said Mrs Benson. 'The nice one facing the Park.'

Sophy took her six months' commercial course and the rebellion that had flared in her when her father vetoed her hopes was damped down. She was accustomed to him being absolute master. There was never any argument with him. He made the rules, providing her with everything she needed and a few things that she didn't—like this commercial course. She often thought that he might have been happier with a son, they might have had more in common. With a daughter he was Victorian, vetting her friends and ordering her life.

The fact that he was head of police, and that he made it his business to know where his daughter was and who she was with twenty-four hours a day, kept the wilder ones of her age group away from her. But she wasn't given the chance to choose for herself, and there were young folk whom she would have liked for friends, and who had nothing against them except boisterous high spirits.

Chief Inspector Brown could cool high spirits with no more than a glance. If Sophy brought friends home he would come into the room and look around as though he was doing a spot check for a Wanted face, giving them all the impression that they were now registered in his mind and that he might be taking their fingerprints from the glasses later.

He was a man to fear. Everyone knew that Sophy Brown's father was stricter than any other father in town, and she got advice all the time on standing up for herself. But the ones who were most scornful about her letting the old man run her life, and telling her what time she had to be in at night and all that rubbish, were the ones who shifted uncomfortably from one foot to the other when they were face to face with him.

When she started work—with a firm of solicitors, the senior partner was a friend of her father's—she was advised by the other girls in the office to leave home and get herself a flat. It was a temptation, but somehow she couldn't break away. She had never seen her father angry, but she was afraid that his anger would be terrible, and she wasn't unhappy.

He showed more concern for her than a lot of fathers did for their children, and when she was nineteen and he died of a heart attack, sitting at his desk, her feeling of loss was overwhelming at first.

She had never thought he could die. He had seemed the most permanent thing in life. She would have expected the house to crumble to dust sooner than her father. But between breakfast and the moment Mr Lowndes took the telephone call, then came out of his office grey-faced, and put an arm around her and said in a choking voice, 'Sophy, dear child,' her father had gone away for ever.

She was proud of him when she read the letters and heard how his friends and colleagues had valued him, but her tears dried after a while because she really felt no closer to him than they did.

He had done what he considered his duty by her, and now she must fend for herself and make her own decisions and mistakes. It was no hardship. Until her father's authority was removed she had never realised how much she resented it. She felt inches taller, as though she really had been tied down with bonds.

It was easy to be decisive because now she could admit what she wanted. She sold the house and she left her job. The house was too big for one, and she had never wanted to be a secretary. She had wanted to go to art school, but that had been two years ago and now she looked around for an apprenticeship in some creative craft.

She left her home town, revelling in her new-found freedom, to learn the art of the potter, and loved every minute of it. She had talent. Working with clay and fire she was in her element, and after eighteen months the woman who owned the pottery and the shop suggested she might like to take on a partnership in the business.

The sale money from the house was sitting in the bank doing nothing and pottery was going to be Sophy's future, there was no other job she wanted to do. But Stewart had opposed the idea.

Sophy was an attractive girl, with dark hair that curled the moment damp air got to it, and blue eyes— Irish colouring from a long way back on her mother's side. Her skin was satin-smooth and soft to touch, and most men wanted to stroke her cheek, to stroke her.

She was small, 'heart-high', she had been called. She looked fragile, but she had never had a day's illness.

Her father would have been surprised how well she could look after herself. She was selective in her friends, and until she met Stewart Baines she hadn't been serious about a man.

She was popular, she was dated, but with Stewart the rapport was immediate, and they came away from the party where they met talking like old friends, but with the excitement of a new and thrilling relationship.

After that he rarely let her out of his sight. She was proud to go around with him because he looked as marvellous as he was. He was six foot tall and ruggedly handsome, struggling to make his way in the overcrowded profession of the theatre, but getting small parts and an occasional TV commercial, and ready for the big break when it came along.

They were together whenever their free time coincided, and life was full and satisfying. She cooked his favourite dishes, he shared a flat with other men, but he had most of his meals with Sophy; and she mended his clothes for him and took his laundry along to the launderette with her own.

When they went to the cinema or the theatre Stewart chose because he knew what was worth seeing, just as he knew the places to eat and the places to go, and Sophy was happy and blooming with love.

He didn't seem to have a single fault, and she was as thrilled as he was about his career. The glamour rubbed off on her, although she preferred the potter's wheel for herself, and she praised him every time he appeared on television, and worried and hoped for him every time he went for an audition.

Then came the evening she told him about Audrey's suggestion about the partnership.

They were in her bedsitter, she had just served supper. She had waited until the food was on the table because she had thought this was exciting news and it would be pleasant to discuss it over a meal. As Stewart took his first mouthful of moussaka she said, 'Audrey asked me today if I'd like to go into partnership with her.'

Stewart looked thoughtful and she explained what she would have to invest. But she knew all about the turnover, her money would be safe, it would be hard to find a better investment. And it would mean she was part-owner instead of employee.

She ended, 'I'd like my own business—well, half a business.'

'Leave it alone,' said Stewart.

'What?'

'You've no worries now. You do your job and pick up your wages.'

She smiled, 'I wouldn't mind a worry or two.'

He reached for her hand across the table and squeezed it and her heart fluttered. 'You worry about me,' he said. 'I don't want you doing the books every evening and getting into a panic about the figures. Tell her to forget it, find somebody else.'

'But I——' Sophy began.

'No,' said Stewart firmly. 'I'll tell her tomorrow if you like.'

'But I want this partnership.'

'More than our partnership?'

She couldn't believe he was serious, but he was. He was telling her that she could lose all they shared if she took that further step in her career, and next day Audrey seemed to have expected it.

Audrey had suggested she should talk it over with Stewart before she made up her mind, and Sophy had been for saying 'Yes' on the spot. When she had to report that Stewart wasn't at all keen Audrey said, 'And you don't want to lose Stewart, do you?'

'Of course I don't.' She loved him, they had wonderful times together.

'And what Stewart says goes,' said Audrey drily. Then she smiled, 'There is somebody else interested, you'll like her, but I wanted to give you first refusal. Don't worry, nothing will change.'

In work very little did change. The new partner was as nice as Audrey said, comfortably middle-aged as she was, and Sophy went on helping in the shop, making her ware in the afternoon. Work didn't change, but other things did.

She had wanted to invest in the pottery, and she was disappointed. The only other disappointment she could remember to compare with this was when her father had stopped her going to art school, and that was how she first recognised the similarity between her father and Stewart.

They were different as could be in every other way, except that they were both tall, but they both gave the orders. They were little dictators, the pair of them, and she was slipping back into the way of life she had known before her father died.

From then on she watched how Stewart made all the decisions, and her happiness slowly faded. When she thought of the future she could only see him growing more like her father and herself becoming more of a shadow or an echo.

She loved him still—well, perhaps it wasn't love any more, but she still found him attractive, but now she began to resent the way he always had to know best.

He was so sure of himself, and one tyrant was enough in any woman's life.

Parting from him would hurt, but she could never discuss anything with him. There was only one point of view on anything. His. He called her 'Baby' and he treated her as though she was a baby, sweet and simple, and it wasn't comforting, it was frightening because sometimes she wondered if he was right.

The final straw came when he suggested they get an apartment together. Her bedsitter was too small for more than one, and there were three other men in his flat, but when he said, 'We should be looking for somewhere we could be together,' she said,

'Oh, I don't know, I'm used to my place.'

'We could get married if you like, no reason why not.' She panicked then, because she felt that if he married her she would be taking his orders for ever. 'When I get back,' he said.

He was off for a month with a touring company, and like a coward she used those weeks to make the break. She bought The Potter's Wheel.

Audrey was sorry to be losing her, and they made arrangements for continuing to sell Sophy's products, but she had told no one else until the last week, when Stewart returned and the balloon went up.

If she hadn't completed every last detail of the deal she knew that he would have stopped her. But it was too late, and he had to accept that she was moving away to start up her own business. He ran the gamut of emotions from fury to—very briefly—pleading. Mostly he raged at her and told her she was every kind of a fool because it was a foregone conclusion that she would end up flat broke.

She should have put the money towards a decent apartment, he said, and why the hell Yorkshire? About as far as she could get. Or was there another man up there? Was she going on her own or moving in with somebody else?

'I'll be on my own,' she said. 'I want to be on my own. I want to do some good work.'

'Making pots?' he sneered and she retorted, stung, 'I create too, you know.'

They had not parted friends. He had told her she wouldn't see him again, except on TV and make no bones about it he was going right to the top there. When she was bankrupt he'd be famous.

Although as she left he had been asking how she could have thrown their relationship away, so he had his memories and his regrets.

She *was* lonely. It was going to be all right here, she would get used to the silence and there would be no one around ordering her about. But she envied Jenine, who had gone hurrying to meet a man who would wait for her.

The men in Sophy's life had never waited for her. She had never defied her father, but if she had done she thought he would have disowned her. And Stewart would soon find another girl, with his looks and his actor's glamour. No, he wouldn't wait.

Her work was going to occupy her for the next few months, but she would meet another man in a little while, and this time she would look out for the danger signs of the petty tyrant. No more male chauvinism for her. She wanted a loving man who respected her needs. She would find one too.

She could almost see him, with a gentle face and a gentle sense of humour. Clever and kind, and living near so that they could spend evenings together, and she could tell him about her days and sit in front of the fire on the sofa with her head on his shoulder and his arm around her.

She wished he was here now so that they could go into the workroom, and she could show him the kiln and the wheel and the workbench. She walked around herself, but she would have to wait for her tools to arrive and get the furniture put into place in the cottage, and the shop organised, before she could light the kiln and get out the clay.

There wasn't much she could do tonight, except lie in her camp bed and watch the pictures in the fire, but it was too early to go to bed and she wasn't tired. She hadn't even brought a book with her.

Perhaps a walk might pass the time and relax her for sleep, and she put on a light camel-coloured cloak, and went out into the empty street. It was brighter by moonlight than it had been by dusk when she'd arrived, and the cobblestones looked like tiny frozen waves. The other shops in the little side street were shuttered and dark.

So was the whole village. After the busy streets she had been used to this was another world. During daytime tourists passed through on their way to the Dales or Scotland, but now the locals were snug at home, with curtains drawn and doors shut.

Sophy met no one at all; she would have to get a dog if it was only for company when she went for a walk. When she came back into her own road she could see the hill, and she was almost sure she could see the grey stones glinting up there.

She still wasn't tired enough for bed, and when she let herself in at the front door she walked straight through and out into the garden. There were signs here of an untended lawn and flower beds, and at the bottom a wooden fence was the boundary between her property and the hill.

Right now it was the hill that interested her. She climbed over the fence and began to trek upwards. It was rough going, of course, but the moonlight showed her the way, and the air was deliciously fresh and cool.

She reached the top scarcely out of breath at all, and with a heady feeling of triumph. Getting to the top of anything was always exhilarating, even if you were alone, and she stood there, getting her bearings, looking around her.

The stones stood between seven and eight feet high, in a horseshoe pattern. The Seven Brothers. She moved from one to the other, tripping light footed between them. 'Hi, fellers,' she said, and was suddenly awestruck into silence, because close to they were eerily impressive.

It must have been a tremendous task hauling them up here and fixing them in their places. If there had been a village down there then what were the houses like, she wondered; and when the people climbed this hill what would happen? Would they pray, or sing and dance, or offer up sacrifices?

She was standing in the centre of the horseshoe and she felt her skin begin to crawl. Sacrifices seemed as likely as anything, and where she was standing was the obvious spot for that kind of carry-on. She was just about to bid the Brothers goodnight when a shadow moved.

She saw it out of the corner of her eye and froze in terror; then she heard the footsteps, soft on the turf, almost inaudible through the soughing of the breeze in the trees. But now she heard them and she turned.

It was a man, and that didn't entirely reassure her. She backed a couple of steps, about to take off fast down the hill, when he demanded, 'What are you doing here?' in a deep voice of such authority that she froze again. 'You're trespassing,' he added.

He was very tall, his shoulders were very broad. Sophy ran her tongue between her lips. 'I was walking, that's all.'

'Not here,' he said. 'Goodnight.'

She had been just about to leave, and you don't argue with strange men at night, where no one could hear if you screamed your head off. She got down the hill as fast as she could, and scrambled over the fence and almost ran into the house.

Who on earth was he, and where had he come from? Maybe I should have counted the Stones, she thought crazily, there might only have been six of them. She could have joked about that if there had been anyone else with her, but alone she could hardly raise a smile.

She stirred the fire into a blaze and told herself again that it would be all right tomorrow. The removal van would arrive and there would be a hundred things to do, and she would ask Jenine who the man was, and why he was walking around the Stones, all alone, up there in the darkness.

CHAPTER TWO

THE removal van arrived early. Sophy had been promised that her goods would be at Halebridge before midday, but she was sweeping out the shop, with the door open, just after ten o'clock, when the van came slowly along the cobbled street.

Jenine was in the kitchen, paper-lining the shelves of the small pantry, and Sophy waved joyfully at the van driver, who was leaning out of his cab window looking for the Potter's Wheel.

'Here we are!' she called.

'And very nice too,' the driver called back, drawing up in front of the shop, and jumping down at her feet.

She was glad he was cheerful, he and his mate. It was nice to have her belongings unloaded with a smile and a joke. They deposited the packing cases in the shop and the workroom, and put down the furniture where she thought she wanted it to be.

She didn't have that much furniture. It had filled her bedsitter to clutter point, but when it was spread out over a living room, a kitchen and a bedroom, there was space to change your mind, and her first thoughts might not be her last. She would enjoy moving things around until she was quite satisfied, and she had all the time in the world ahead.

But the delivery men put everything where she indicated and had a cup of coffee each and half a packet of wholemeal biscuits when everything was out of the van, pocketed their tip and the cheque for the account, and wished her good luck.

She and Jenine waved them off, and then got down to unpacking the cases of pottery and filling the shelves in the shop.

Once Sophy got into production she had no doubts about her ability to keep her own shop stocked, to send a steady supply to Audrey and—with luck—to other shops that were looking for inexpensive attractive ware.

Jenine was enchanted by a collection of assorted jugs on which Sophy had painted cat motifs. All kinds of cats, from snoozing domestic tabbies to prowling jungle tigers. No two were quite alike and each had charm and character.

'Are you fond of cats?' she asked.

'Yes,' said Sophy. 'I was thinking last night that I needed a cat. Or a dog. I think I'd rather have a dog because you can take a dog for a walk, so if you hear of a puppy that needs a home——'

She lifted out a glazed earthenware casserole. 'By the way,' she said, 'I was walking last night, up the hill to the Stones, and I met a man who ordered me off. Who is he?'

Jenine's mouth went tight. She took a little while to answer and then she snapped, 'Oh, him!' That didn't tell Sophy much, except that Jenine didn't like him. 'Robert Carlton,' added Jenine as though that should explain everything, but it didn't.

'So who's Robert Carlton?' Sophy asked.

'Halebridge Agricultural Equipment, you must have seen the name.' Sophy had heard of it. The factory was about five miles away in New Halebridge, a small town that had grown up around it. 'You must have seen him too, he's been on television often enough. One of our leading industrialists,' Jenine added quite bitterly.

'Does he own the top of the hill?' Sophy asked, and Jenine put down a cat jug, carefully and silently as though if she spoke at the same time she might have banged it down and cracked it. Then she said,

'He owns the hill. He owns half the village, nearly everybody around here works for him. My sister does, and her husband.'

'He doesn't own this place.' This was all Sophy's.

'He owns our house. The whole row. Oh, he's the big man around here.'

'What's the matter with him?' Sophy enquired. 'Except too much property.'

Jenine dug down again, into the plastic packing granules in the large box, and came up like a lucky dip with a stack of bowls. 'He's David's brother,' she said.

'David?' Sophy echoed, but she had guessed who David was before Jenine explained,

'My boy-friend.'

Jenine hadn't discussed her man, except last night when she had said he would wait for her. Neither girl had talked much about herself, there hadn't been that much time. Sophy knew Jenine had worked in this shop for four years, apparently without any urge to try her hand on the production side.

The husband and wife from whom Sophy took over had recommended her. She lived with her widowed father, and Sophy had felt that she and Jenine would get along together.

'David's an engineer,' said Jenine proudly. 'He's awfully clever.'

'Uhuh?' said Sophy encouragingly, and that was all Jenine needed to start the confidences coming. David

was the greatest. They had been going around together for about two months now, and he was absolutely super. Tall and dark—she brought out a snapshot of a very personable young man in swimming
trunks, lolling on a sandy beach, with no clue as to
where the beach was, just sea and sand.

'On holiday last month,' Jenine sighed, and smiled
blissfully as though she could feel the sun on her face
again and the sand between her bare toes. 'Near More-
cambe,' she said.

'I thought it might be a desert island,' Sophy smiled,
and Jenine grimaced,

'Some chance! Robert wouldn't wear that.'

'What do you mean?' They were talking about a
man who looked like an intelligent normal adult
male, so what business was it of his brother's where he
spent his holidays? 'What's it got to do with Robert?'
Sophy asked.

'You don't know Robert.'

'I don't want to, but how could he stop David going
abroad?'

'He wouldn't want him going on holiday with *me*.
We can slip off if it's only for a weekend or a day or
two, but if Robert thought that we were serious he'd
raise a real fuss.'

'Why?'

'We're too young. He says.'

'How old is David?' You couldn't always tell from a
snapshot. He could be eighteen or nineteen perhaps,
although he didn't look younger than Jenine's twenty
years.

When she said, 'Twenty-two,' Sophy almost dropped
the photograph.

'He's well past the age of consent, then,' she said, 'so
what's his brother's beef?'

'We're too young,' Jenine repeated, 'and two months isn't long enough to know each other. And he does have this influence over David. He sort of brought him up, after their mother was killed in a car crash. He's much older than David, they're half-brothers really, David's name's Irving, and David's always looked to Robert for everything, and Robert is against young marriages.'

'Oh,' said Sophy, after all that, delivered breathily. 'Is Robert married?'

'No.'

'So what does he consider the right age? Forty? Fifty?'

Jenine's eyes filled with tears and Sophy was shocked at her own tactlessness and the tartness in her voice. It didn't say much for Jenine's happiness if David was letting his brother dictate to him about this. But it wasn't Sophy's business, and that sort of remark was bound to hurt.

'I'm sorry,' she said. 'It's just that I had a father like that. I wasn't twenty-two, I was nineteen when he died, but he'd messed my life about and it just makes me so angry.'

She wouldn't tell her about Stewart, not just yet, but she was sorry to meet another girl whose happiness was being threatened. She asked gently, 'What could his brother do anyway?'

'David works for him. He's very rich.' Jenine's eyelids drooped, as though she hated admitting this, and it didn't put David in too good a light. 'And that's the way David's used to living. Robert's generous.' Her father had been generous, so long as she'd obeyed him in everything. 'David says if we don't rush things he'll come round, and I think he will.' She smiled uncertainly, asking for reassurance.

'Do you see much of him?' Sophy asked. 'Robert, I mean.'

'No. He comes down into the village, but he never says much to me.'

'Where do they live?'

'On top of the hill.'

Sophy gasped, remembering the isolation and the darkness up there last night. 'But there isn't anything on top of the hill, except the Stones. And trees.'

'There's a house.' Jenine was stripping the protective newspaper off the bowls and stacking them on the shelf. 'It's hidden by the trees. Unless the lights are on you can't see it, and then only in winter time. It's a lovely house.' She sounded wistful. 'Not that I've been asked in.'

Sophy was feeling less happy about Jenine's love affair by the minute. She wasn't too happy about the house up there either. The Stones she hadn't minded, she quite liked the Stones, but a house in the little wood, owned by a man she was already disliking heartily, was a blot on the skyline.

'Do you have a special boy-friend?' Jenine was asking her.

'No. I did, but not now.' Sophy looked at her shelves that were filling. 'Now I've got this, and I'd better make a go of it, because all my money's here.'

'You made all these?' Jenine's glance covered the same ground.

'Yes.'

'You're very good, aren't you?'

From learning to throw functional pots Sophy had progressed until now everything she made had her own flair: sometimes in shape, sometimes in decoration, sometimes in the clever use of glaze and colour.

'Thank you,' she said.

'I just want to be a housewife,' sighed Jenine. 'Oh, I like working in the shop, but really I want to be married and have children and look after them and my husband. I've never wanted a career.'

Jenine should have met Stewart, who disliked ambitious women, except that he didn't particularly like children.

'I just want David,' she said, and blushed prettily. 'I don't usually talk like this. I don't go around telling people that Robert's against David seeing me. Once you start that kind of gossip in a village——' she pulled a face.

'Don't they know?' Sophy asked. 'Don't people know?'

'We've been seen together.' Jenine was still holding the smallest bowl. She turned it slowly in her hands, looking down at the fish painted at the very bottom. 'But nobody thinks it's serious.'

'But it is?'

'Yes.' She repeated, '*Yes.*'

Sophy felt that she should be flattered. She was being trusted with a confidence, although if she had been asked for advice, and dared to give it, she would have admitted that things didn't sound very reassuring. 'You won't say anything, will you?' Jenine asked anxiously.

'Of course I won't. I don't know anyone but you round here.'

Jenine nodded, satisfied, and they went on with the unpacking.

By the end of the day everything was in place, and after she had eaten her evening meal Sophy phoned Audrey. 'We were just going to call you,' said Audrey. 'Did you find everything all right?'

'It's lovely.' And so it was now. She was sitting on

her little Victorian sofa, covered in red plush with patchwork scatter cushions, and the room glowed in the firelight. 'I'm starting work tomorrow,' she said, 'but I just wanted to tell you I've settled in.'

She phoned several other friends. They all said they'd been going to phone her, and she was sure they would have done, although maybe not tonight. They were living busy lives, they weren't sitting about with their feet up and all this peace around them. Until just a few days ago she hadn't had a moment to spare herself, and the change of tempo was a whole new way of life.

She didn't phone Stewart. She would have been safe enough from this distance, but she didn't think he was waiting to hear from her, and she was right. The second girl she rang told her that he had been telling them all that his affair with Sophy had run its course; which was very true, but showed he was making a quick recovery. His pride obviously mattered more to him than Sophy did, and she had known that and she was glad she had got away.

She was a little worried about Jenine. She had been used to confiding in Audrey; maybe that was how Jenine saw her, as an Audrey figure, employer and older and wiser in the ways of the world. But Audrey was in her fifties, and Sophy was twenty-one, and she didn't feel equipped to deal with anybody else's problems.

The only way she had dealt with her own so far was to run away from Stewart, and if her father hadn't died she might well have been a secretary still, or married to a man of his choice. She couldn't imagine herself ever standing up to her father.

Jenine seemed a gentle girl, and between David and his brother she could be badly hurt. Perhaps it was safer to be without a man in your life unless a very kind one came along. But Sophy was already needing somebody to talk to in the evenings, and if nobody wanted a good home for a puppy or a kitten she would just have to go out and buy one.

A dog couldn't settle your problems, but saying them aloud might help, if it was only, 'What shall we have for supper tomorrow?'

She didn't take a walk tonight. She had her comfortable bed upstairs, and some paperback novels that had come in the removal van, and she snuggled happily between the sheets. When she settled for sleep the silence didn't bother her, and she slept soundly.

The Potter's Wheel opened next day. There were three shops in this side street—the others were a grocer's and a small children's boutique—and several customers came in. Some were locals who wanted to see how the ware had changed from the previous potters, and to see the new girl; but some were ready to buy and Jenine was a good salesgirl.

After a while Sophy left her and went into the workroom. That was where she was happiest. She put on a smock over her jeans and checked shirt, and rolled up her sleeves, and took a plastic bag containing a lump of clay out of a packing case.

She was going to start by making some mugs. Mugs were cheap and cheerful, and good sellers, and they'd help her to get the feel of her wheel. It was electric, like the one she had used in Audrey's workroom, but this was her own and she couldn't wait to start on it.

She wedged the clay by hand, tearing off small lumps and banging them together to force out the air, working it soft and even in texture. Then she began to knead it on the workbench, slowly and rhythmically.

When the door opened and Jenine looked in Sophy grinned at her, she was enjoying herself, but Jenine's expression cut the grin short. 'What's happened?' Sophy asked, with a sinking heart.

'Robert Carlton's here.' Jenine gulped as she spoke.

'What does he want?'

'To see you.' Jenine gulped again. 'It couldn't be about David and me, could it?'

That would be uppermost in Jenine's mind, but Sophy could see no possible reason why Robert Carlton should involve a stranger in a family affair. 'Of course not,' she said.

'Are you coming?'

'Send him in here.'

Sophy wasn't taking off her smock and wiping her hands, and going into the shop as though her work could wait while she attended to him. Besides, there might be others in the shop and this might possibly be a private matter.

Jenine was looking flurried as she hurried away, and Sophy gave the clay another push, lift and twist. This always calmed her, she always felt in control while she was working. She heard the door open again, but she didn't look up for about three seconds, and then she had a steady if cool smile on her face.

The smile stiffened as she met his eyes. For a moment she felt as shocked as though someone had punched her just below the heart, and she drew in her breath almost painfully.

'Good morning, Miss Brown,' he said.

She knew him. In the moonlight that night she had only had a general impression of a big man who was angry with her, but now she saw him clearly. He had her father's piercing eyes beneath the heavy brows and Stewart's aura of male arrogance. He looked like a

combination of everything that had inhibited and
humbled her.

He was probably stronger than either of them, he
was certainly richer. Her father's power had been limited and Stewart had no power yet, but Robert Carlton
owned half Halebridge, and probably half New Halebridge as well, nearly everybody round here worked
for him, and look what he was doing to his brother
and poor Jenine.

Sophy felt as though she was face to face with a
nightmare, although he was a striking-looking man.
She said, 'Good morning,' still kneading the clay with
fingers that felt rubbery. So did her legs. It was a wonder she was still standing upright. 'What can I do for
you?' she managed to say.

'I didn't realise who you were the other night.' His
voice was deeper than her father's, he had a broader
chest, wider shoulders. He said, 'I've come to apologise
for ordering you off the hill.'

He wasn't smiling while he apologised, but he was
watching her with those eyes that probed into your
mind and made you drop your own gaze and look
away. 'Doesn't it belong to you?' she said.

'Yes, but my neighbours are welcome to walk there.
And tourists in daylight. After dark I don't encourage
strangers.'

She smiled, briefly, at the clay she was working. 'I
could hardly have got up to anything very outrageous,
could I? I was alone.'

'It's hardly the place for lovemaking, if that's what
you're talking about.' Too open to the elements, too
chilly by night, but she supposed that was what she
meant and she was surprised to find herself blushing.
'But it does seem to hold a fascination after dark for
the lunatic fringe,' he said.

'And you thought that was me?' She opened wide eyes. 'Thank you. What was I supposed to be doing? Calling up the spirits of the Stones? Doing my own black magic thing?'

'You seemed to be dancing around,' he said drily. 'I thought you were either drunk or drugged.'

'*What?*' He didn't apologise for that mistake and she remembered herself skipping from Stone to Stone, her cloak flapping about her. She had thought he could have been hewn from the same rock as the Stones and she still thought that. A rock-like man, with a heart of granite. Oh, she knew him, she was intimately conversant with his kind.

'How long have you owned the Stones?' she asked. 'I'd have thought they'd have been public property by now, unless you claim ancestry going back to Stone Age man.'

'Don't we all?' he said. 'But my family has held the land for the last two hundred years. Good morning, Miss Brown.'

Jenine came in about five minutes later, pale and apprehensive, and Sophy said, 'He said he hadn't realised I was a law-abiding local. I have his gracious permission to walk on his hill, even after dark.'

'That was all?'

'Yes.'

Jenine smiled, in relief it seemed. 'He scares me,' she confessed.

'Why doesn't David stand up to him?' The times her friends had asked her that when she was a teenager, but David was no teenaged girl, he was a man, and this was a very different matter.

'He thinks it's better if we play it cool.' Jenine picked up a small piece of clay and rolled it with a forefinger in the palm of her other hand. 'After a while he thinks Robert will come round.'

'Super,' said Sophy. 'And if he doesn't?' It was tough, asking Jenine that, but she had just faced the fact that her own love affair had no future, and although she was sad she was freer and stronger. Deceiving yourself was a risky business.

'Then we get married anyway,' said Jenine.

'That's all right, then,' said Sophy.

'But don't tell anyone, will you?'

'Of course not.' She hoped it would work out all right, but she still didn't like the sound of it.

Next day she found her dog, in some postcard ads stuck up in the post office. 'Wanted, good home for adorable cross-bred puppies. Mother Border collie.' There was a phone number, and when Sophy rang she was told she was lucky because they'd all gone but one and she could see him any time.

She drove over after work, to a farm about three miles away, and came into the yard behind a herd of cows who had filled the lane in front of her for the past ten minutes. She was in no hurry, she hadn't tried to pass them, she had wondered if the dog helping to shepherd the cows was the mother of her puppy. It certainly looked an intelligent animal.

When the cowman went to close the gate she called, 'If this is Leas Farm'—which it was, there was a board on a post saying so—'can I come in? I've come about the puppy.'

The cows were heading for the milking sheds and she sat in her car until there was a clear path to the house, then she got out and went over and pulled the ring on the end of a chain by the door.

A bell clanged and a woman appeared. 'I'm Sophy Brown,' Sophy began. The woman beamed,

'Here he is, he's waiting for you.'

A large bewhiskered head came round the door, and Sophy goggled at it. 'That's a *puppy*?'

'He's about five months,' the woman explained. She patted his head and she hardly had to bend down. 'Nobody wanted him. We didn't bother to take the notice down.' She added as though she was still surprised about it, 'The others were really pretty little things.'

'What was his father?'

'We don't know.'

Sophy found herself giggling, because this one was a real mix-up. He had long curly hair, long tails, long legs and long ears, a black coat and a black and white face. Right now his tail was swishing and his tongue was lolloping as he panted what might have been a welcome.

'Is he friendly?' she asked.

'Oh yes,' said the woman, 'he's a lovely lad. We'd have kept him, but we've got three already, and four cats.'

So that was it, he was Sophy's. He didn't have a name, he'd been 'the puppy'. The woman said, 'Goodbye, puppy, behave yourself now.'

The man who had driven the cows in opened the gate for her, and grinned at the dog who was sprawled all over the back seat. 'Shall you be showing him at Crufts?'

'What as?' said Sophy.

There was a great deal of panting as she drove along, and she was glad to get home and get him out of the car. He had no collar or lead and the only way she could guide him into the house was by the scruff of the neck, her fingers in his long curly coat. If he had taken it into his head to make a break that could well have been the last of him so far as she was concerned, he seemed a very strong dog, but he let her lead him in. Although the moment she closed the door into the street he took off wildly down the little hall.

The farm had been a big rambling old house, and of course there had been plenty of space around it. 'I do hope you're not claustrophobic,' Sophy called after him; he was rushing round the living room now, he looked much bigger in her house, 'and I do hope you're not going to grow any more!'

She had no idea at what age dogs stopped growing but, now she realised that he was as tall as the sofa seat, she began to feel that perhaps she should have made enquiries. He *looked* fully grown. If he wasn't she dreaded to think what size he might end up.

He sat down at last and eyed her expectantly. He was probably hungry. She had a packet of puppy meal in, a packet of dog biscuits and a couple of tins of dog food, and she opened a tin of the meat, mixed it with meal and put it down on the kitchen floor.

She watched amazed as he despatched it in seconds, then sat up, licking his whiskery chops with an expression that said, 'Fine for a first course, where's the meal?'

'I can see you're going to be expensive!' She emptied some biscuits in the bowl and he crunched them with fine strong teeth. 'And what am I going to call you?'

One eye had a white eye-patch and she said 'Patch?' trying it out for sound. He went on crunching, Patch rang no bells with him. 'Rover? Curly? Dopey? Prince?' He took no notice at all and she laughed; he was rather a comic. 'What I wanted was a nice little puppy,' she told him, and his ears lifted, he looked up and his tail wagged. 'Puppy?' she repeated, the swishing tail answered her and, incredibly, he grinned. 'So that's got to be your name?' It *was* his name. It was no use telling him that in future he should answer to Prince.

'I suppose it's no sillier than Stewart calling me Baby,' she said, and a wave of loneliness swept over her, so that she reached to stroke the dog, because he was alive and warm and near.

The phone rang, making her jump. If this was Stewart it was a coincidence, just when she was thinking about him. She went to answer it, torn between reluctance and anticipation, and when Audrey said, 'Hello,' she didn't know whether she was disappointed or not.

'Everything still all right?' asked Audrey.

'Yes, I've started working and we've had quite a few sales.'

'Good. About sales. A man came in this afternoon from your part of the world. He's got a shop in Whitby and he was quite taken with your cat jugs. He said he thought they'd go well and he'd like to talk to you about it. He's on holiday now, he'll be back on the fifteenth. Here's the number.'

Sophy searched in her bureau for a pencil and paper and wrote down the figures, with the phone tucked into her shoulder. 'Can you hear heavy breathing?' Audrey asked suddenly, and Sophy laughed.

'It isn't on the line, it's here. I've bought a dog.' Puppy had his paws on the open flap of the bureau and was standing on his hind legs, his face close to Sophy's.

'What is it?' Audrey sounded slightly alarmed. 'A St Bernard?'

'You could be half right,' said Sophy. 'I must be crazy, I wanted a *little* dog.' She looked at him, looking at her, and laughed again. 'I don't know though, I'm growing quite attached to him and we've only been together half an hour.'

Jenine had known that Sophy was off to collect a puppy after work, and she asked as she walked into the shop at nine o'clock next morning, 'Did you get him?'

'He's in the kitchen.' Sophy looked towards the door leading to the hall of the house.

'Can I see him?'

'Of course, but I warn you he's not quite what I expected.'

Jenine went to see, and came back looking as apprehensive as she had when she'd announced that Robert Carlton was waiting in the shop. 'He's a big dog,' she commented.

'He didn't seem quite so big at the farm,' said Sophy. 'Perhaps it was because I'd been driving behind a herd of cows for ten minutes.'

'What?' Jenine didn't get the connection. She said, 'He'll need a lot of exercise.'

'He'll get me out in the evenings,' Sophy agreed. She'd bought him now. He was her reponsibility, feeding and exercising. She bought some scrag ends from the butcher, and begged some bones; and a dog collar and lead from another shop in the high street.

Puppy let her put on the collar but showed a strong reluctance to being pulled by the lead. When Sophy stepped outside with him he charged up the road, although she had tried for the opposite direction, and went at such a pace that she was hustled into a jog-trot, calling to Jenine for help.

Two of them holding the lead were just about a match for him, but she couldn't see Jenine wanting to spend her evenings helping Puppy get his exercise.

She took him into the garden that evening and he

raced around for half an hour or so before he showed signs of flagging. She had hoped to mow the lawn and dig up the weeds and plant the flower beds, but for a while this looked like being Puppy's stamping ground.

'Heel!' Sophy called when he stopped running, tempting him with chocolate drops, and he came. She walked around with him. She was walking with him rather than he with her, and although he usually came when she called she wouldn't risk him outside the garden just yet. But he was no fool. He should be trainable. Tomorrow, in the garden, she'd try the lead again.

Next day she worked late in the workroom, nursing the kiln up to the right temperature for firing and preparing a glaze for tomorrow. She had let Puppy out and in from the garden several times during the day. He was taking to his new home and proving more sensible than he looked.

He lay down on the workshop floor and snoozed while she worked, and when the glaze was right, not too thick nor too thin, and she was through in here, they ate their evening meal together.

She was glad she had him, he was company, even if she did have to exercise him as soon as she had finished eating. She put on her cloak and took a torch; it was dark by now and if she was going to run round and round the garden with Puppy she wanted to see the bushes and the two gnarled old apple trees.

She had thought he was quite safe and secure in the garden, with thick bramble hedges either side and the fence at the bottom, but as soon as she let him out he loped off towards the fence and wriggled through the horizontal slats. It was the hill he fancied. He had obviously done this before, when she'd let him out earlier, and found the wider slopes of the hill more to his liking than a small overgrown garden.

Sophy sat on top of the fence and called him and he waited for her. That was something, that he hadn't gone dashing off, and she did have permission to walk here, and there wasn't much damage he could do. There were no sheep he might be chasing and he could hardly harm the Stones.

'Oh, all right,' she sighed, and swung herself over. The hill *was* a better idea than the garden, it meant he could really run, but he kept her as his pivot point and raced back to her again and again. Over the hill were the Dales, but so long as they kept to 'their' side, and the plateau on top, they weren't likely to get lost.

She climbed, as she had a few nights ago, feeling by now that it was nearly a familiar path, and that she could half recognise the bigger tufts of grass and the formation of some of the stones underfoot. Somewhere there would be a real path, probably a drive up to the house, but here it was rough turf.

Puppy was at the top first, which wasn't surprising. Sophy had read that animals were particularly sensitive to the atmosphere of mysterious places like this, and she was relieved that he didn't sit down and howl. That would have been a bit too spooky.

He didn't seem very interested in the Stones at all, it was the wood—all those trees—that he preferred, and once Sophy was up on the plateau he trotted into the fringe of trees.

She called him again, but softly, she still felt a little awestruck up here, then she switched on her torch and followed him. The house was just through there. She could see the lights, and she was curious. She wondered what kind of house it was that Jenine had described as 'lovely'.

It was, rather. It was old grey stone, with thick stone-slate roof, a sprawling shape, with dormer windows, and on this side the wood grew very close. Puppy was literally snuffling along a flower bed under one of the windows, and if he should decide to start digging there, or barking, Sophy could be in trouble. 'Heel, you idiot!' she hissed at him.

He took no notice at all and she ducked out of the shelter of the trees to get to him. She could see straight into the room, there were several side lamps burning.

It was a sitting room, and if she dared she would have loved to stop and stare. It was beautiful, and so was the woman sitting there. Her hair shone like red gold, and she was wearing something that flowed around her, a caftan or a loose sort of dress in a colour between green and blue, a kingfisher colour.

Sophy saw the broad back of Robert Carlton. He was standing by a table, the girl was looking at him, talking to him, and it was all absolutely fascinating; and she had better get out of here pretty darn quick.

She clutched Puppy's collar and hauled him back into the trees. He didn't object, he was quite amenable and he didn't mind going back home either. He raced down the hill as happily as he had raced up it.

Next day Sophy asked Jenine, 'Who lives in the Carlton house besides Robert and David?'

They were drinking a mid-morning cup of coffee in the workroom, with the door into the shop open in case customers arrived. 'Mrs Tewson,' said Jenine. 'She's the housekeeper. And Miss Harris.'

'Who's Miss Harris?'

'She works there.'

'Is she a gorgeous redhead?'

'Huh?' Jenine's brow wrinkled. 'She's about fifty.'

'It wasn't her, then,' said Sophy. 'But I took Puppy walking on the hill last night, and we finished up outside the house.' Jenine's mouth formed a perfect O.

'The lights were on,' said Sophy, 'and I could see into one of the rooms and I saw this fantastic-looking girl. And our Robert.'

'Did they see you?' Jenine croaked, and Sophy grinned,

'No, thank goodness. It was a bit of a cheek, wasn't it? But I really didn't stop to think. Do you know who she is?'

Jenine gave a prim little shrug. 'One of Robert's girls, I suppose.'

'How many does he have?'

'They say there's safety in numbers,' said Jenine tartly, then she added, 'He nearly got married once.'

'What happened?' Sophy asked, because Jenine was expecting her to show interest, and Jenine said in the hushed tones of someone digging up old bones,

'That's part of the trouble, David says. Even David doesn't know what really happened, but it made Robert very cynical.'

'How long ago was all this?'

From Jenine's expression it was history. 'Oh, a *long* time ago. Robert's—oh, more than ten years older than David. David was away at school. It was after their mother died.'

That was a tragedy, their mother and David's father —Robert's stepfather—being killed in a motorway fog pile-up. When she'd heard about that Sophy had felt very sorry for David, who was no more than a child at the time; but she had less sympathy to spare for this long-ago love affair that had turned Robert into a marriage-hater.

She drained her coffee cup and said, 'From my experience men like Robert Carlton are born, not made. I'd like to meet the woman who's supposed to have changed his life, and hear her side of the story.'

'Would you like to meet David?' Jenine asked suddenly.

'That would be nice.'

'You're the only one I've told about us, that it's serious.'

Jenine must have been longing for someone to confide in and Sophy was an outsider yet, the safest girl in the village, so far as secrets went. 'Come to tea,' invited Sophy. 'How about Sunday?'

It seemed that Sunday suited, and on Sunday afternoon Jenine brought David Irving along for tea.

Sophy had put on quite a spread. Since she came here she hadn't had the time to bother with fancy cooking. It was only when she began to plan what she would give her guests that she realised she had missed providing meals for Stewart. She had often had small dinner parties in her bedsitter, but Puppy wasn't a fussy eater so long as there was plenty of it. It was a come-down, from a man to cook for nearly every day, and friends usually once a week at least, to a dog and herself.

So she spent most of Sunday morning happily baking. Jenine was quite taken aback at the display of food, and Sophy laughed, 'I'm keeping my hand in. Living alone you don't bother. You're my housewarming party.'

The young man who had come in with Jenine was recognisable from his snapshot on the beach. Fully clad now in a well cut grey suit, a very pale pink shirt and a pink and grey tie, he looked a touch dandyish. But his grin was attractive and he was certainly good-looking, with no feature that Sophy could see that linked him with his half-brother.

'Hello,' he said. 'I've been looking forward to meeting you. Jenine tells me you make the most splendid pottery.'

'That's because she's a splendid salesgirl and my pots are what she's selling,' smiled Sophy. 'Now, do have a drink, both of you.'

She had stocked her drinks cupboard especially for them. The choice was limited, but they both settled for sherry and David proposed a toast to the success of The Potter's Wheel under its new management.

As Sophy had left London to come here, and David knew London well, that was what they talked about for a while. He struck Sophy as a man about town rather than a countryman, and Jenine sat quietly, looking at him with adoring eyes.

'But you work down here, don't you?' asked Sophy, over the tea table. 'At the New Halebridge works?'

'At my brother's works?' He spoke with ironic reverence. 'Of course I do,' he said. 'He's boss as well as brother, believe me.'

'Sophy says her father was just like him,' said Jenine suddenly, and David grinned as though he was greeting a fellow sufferer.

'He *was*? I didn't think there was another. Welcome to the club. How did you deal with him?'

'He died,' said Sophy quietly and David sobered.

'I'm sorry. There's a great deal to be said for them, the power men. Robert's a brother in a million, and a boss in a million.' The admiration seemed genuine. Then he smiled wryly, 'But he will be boss, you know.'

'Oh, I do know,' said Sophy, with feeling.

'He's packing me off to Canada for six months. Did Jenine tell you?'

She hadn't. 'Don't you want to go?' Sophy asked.

'Not particularly.' He took another flapjack, and Jenine poured him another cup of tea and he laughed. 'But what I want isn't going to make a blind bit of difference.'

They stayed until about ten o'clock, it was a successful if small housewarming and Puppy ate all the sausage rolls that were left over.

For the next couple of weeks Sophy worked in the workroom, building up her stocks. She phoned the number Audrey had given her and was answered by a pleasant-voiced man who ordered three dozen assorted jugs to see how they went. He'd come along and collect them, he said.

She *was* busy. She hardly left the house, except to buy food or exercise Puppy. The times she had climbed that hill, which was definitely Puppy's favourite playground, but she had managed to impress on him that it was out of bounds beyond the first trees. The Stones were as far as they went, and so far they hadn't met any of the 'lunatic fringe' after dark.

If they did Puppy was a big dog. Sophy was trying to convince herself he wasn't getting bigger, but she had an uneasy suspicion that he was. She asked Jenine, 'Do you think he's still growing?' and Jenine said,

'He might be, yes.'

Jenine was pensive these days, because David was leaving soon. That was Robert's fault, of course. Robert thought that if David and Jenine were parted six months it would all fizzle out, but he was wrong. They were getting engaged before David went. She told Sophy that, under the seal of secrecy too, but the time came nearer and there was still no ring.

When David was due off tomorrow Sophy was very

concerned about Jenine. Sales were good, but between customers she tended to stand and stare wistfully into space.

As yet Sophy had had no time to make any other friends. Folk said good morning and good afternoon to her, but she was very much the newcomer, and there was nobody with whom she could discuss Jenine's dilemma.

Not that she would have broken a confidence, but she would have liked to know what Jenine's family and friends thought about this.

It was serious to Jenine all right, but was it to David? He had not struck Sophy as anxious to take on commitments. Had he really said that he and Jenine would get engaged before he went, or was that hopeful thinking on her part? And if he didn't hand over a ring tonight, what state was Jenine likely to be in tomorrow, and for quite a few tomorrows?

Sophy suggested, 'While David's away why don't you use the time? I could teach you how to be a potter. It's a craft that can make a good living, and it's fun.'

'No, thank you,' said Jenine sweetly. 'I'll have plenty to do, I don't need a career.'

You may be needing something, thought Sophy, and when Jenine went that evening Sophy watched her through the shop window, remembering her running footsteps on the cobblestones that first night almost a month ago.

She was almost running now, off home to make herself beautiful, to meet David Irving, who was supposed to be waiting for her with the ring in his pocket.

'What do you think?' Sophy asked Puppy. He *was* getting bigger. In three weeks his head was definitely higher, measured against the counter. 'I don't think we're going to hear very good news in the morning,' said Sophy.

But Jenine was back that night. Sophy was washing up after her evening meal when the house doorbell rang and it was Jenine asking, 'Can I use the phone?'

'Of course.'

'The kiosk's out of order.'

She followed Sophy into the living room and darted across to the phone, while Sophy went back into the kitchen, closing the door behind her.

She guessed that David hadn't turned up and Jenine was trying to contact him, and she sighed, finished washing her plate, tipped the water down the sink and stripped off her rubber gloves.

Jenine came slowly into the kitchen. 'Robert answered,' she said, 'so I hung up.'

'David didn't come?' Jenine shook her head. 'Come and sit down.' Sophy led her back to the sofa by the fire. 'I'll get you a drink. There might be a very good reason.'

'Robert,' said Jenine bitterly.

'Perhaps. But if David doesn't want to get engaged at the moment it doesn't mean he doesn't care for you. I know you'll feel rotten about it, but maybe you do need that six months to be quite sure.' Sophy poured a little brandy into a glass. 'I thought I was in love,' she said. 'It ended the week before I came down here, and there's no future with Stewart for me.'

After a moment Jenine said huskily, 'But you're not pregnant, are you?'

That was a complication. That altered things. Sophy gave her the glass and waited while she sipped a little. Then she asked, 'Does David know?'

'I wanted him to give me the ring before I told him.'

'I don't know what to say.' Brisk little pep talks

would be out of place, so would reminding Jenine that other girls' love affairs had ended. 'I only wish there was something I could do.'

'Oh, but there is.' Jenine was looking at her with piteous eagerness. 'Oh, *please*, Sophy, would you go up to the house and talk to Robert?'

CHAPTER THREE

'TALK to Robert? Don't you mean David?' Sophy asked, and Jenine's earnest look became even more intense.

'Robert,' she insisted. 'It all depends on him, you see, he could take everything away from David.'

That depends on your priorities, thought Sophy. There were a great many things Robert couldn't take away, but David didn't seem to be setting much value on them.

She asked, 'Now what could I say to Robert?' Men like Robert Carlton weren't swayed by appeals. It would be like requesting one of the Stones to move a little to the left, please, although Jenine was hiccuping,

'You could tell him that we do love each other, it is the real thing.'

She looked heartbreakingly appealing, her mascara smudged and her eyes swimming in desperate tears. 'Why me?' Sophy wanted no part in it. 'Why don't *you* go up there and ask to see David?' But she had to offer, 'I'll come with you if you like.'

Jenine turned her face away, her shoulders shaking. 'I c-can't. I'd just make a fool of myself. I can't go up there!'

'It isn't Dracula's castle.' Jenine was spilling the brandy on the sofa and Sophy took the glass from her as she sobbed, 'I couldn't face Robert.'

'Forget Robert. This is David's problem.'

And Sophy could imagine what the next six months

would be like if David flew off to Canada unenlightened and uncommitted. Jenine wouldn't be much help in the shop, that was for sure. There would be dramas and tears and probably breakages, and there wasn't time to find anyone else to go looking for David Irving.

He might not be at home anyway. 'What's the number?' she asked, picking up the phone.

Jenine mumbled it automatically and then protested, 'You can't talk about this to Robert over the phone.'

'I'm trying to get David.'

She got the engaged signal. She made Jenine finish what was left of the brandy and then tried again, and it was still engaged. 'All right,' she said, 'I'll go to the house. I won't talk to Robert. It wouldn't do any good if I did—I remember trying to talk to my father—and Stewart—and those kind of men don't even hear you. But I will find out where David is. He might just have been delayed, have you thought of that?'

'Two hours?' Jenine whimpered.

'There could have been a business hold-up, there must be all sorts of last-minute briefings and arrangements. Anyhow, I'll find where he is and then if you can't see him you can phone him, and for goodness' sake *tell* him.'

'Oh, I will,' Jenine promised fervently.

Sophy tried to leave Puppy behind, but he shoved his way past her out of the kitchen door, and was down the garden and through the fence in a flash.

Ah well, she thought, he's getting some pleasure out of it. She was hating the role that had been forced on her. She didn't want to have to track David down, she didn't want to be left with Jenine sobbing on her shoulder. Jenine had a father and a married sister, but as she had emphasised all along how terribly secret her affair was it was possible that even the family didn't know she was pregnant.

There was going to be a real scandal here, especially as the father was David Irving, and if she could contact David Sophy would allow herself the luxury of blowing her top. Somebody should tell him how selfish he was.

Puppy was delighted that it was all right to go through the little wood tonight, and he was ahead of her when she reached the house, returning to the flower bed that had intrigued him last time. 'Get your big feet off the flowers!' she hissed at him. She was edgy enough without having to apologise for Puppy's meanderings.

There were lights on, but tonight curtains were drawn across the window of the room where she had seen the striking redhaired girl and Robert Carlton, and she had to find a door, not a window. She rounded the corner and reached the front of the house from which a tarmac drive curved down the hill. The dark oak front door was closed and the knocker was heavy when she lifted it, a black circle of wrought-iron 'rope'.

After a couple of knocks she noticed the bell, and pushed that instead. She must have sounded very impatient, because the woman who answered demanded, 'Whatever is it?'

Mrs Tewson, the housekeeper. This was the first time Sophy had seen her, but she was dressed for the part in a neat navy woollen dress.

'Could I see Mr Irving, please?' Sophy asked, and saw Robert Carlton coming down the hall.

He said, 'It's all right, Mrs Tewson,' and Mrs Tewson moved away and Robert Carlton filled the doorway. He looked down at Sophy and then at Puppy. 'Miss Brown, isn't it?'

'Yes.'

'Come in.' She followed him down the hall into the room she had seen through the window. For some reason the fact that she had peered in here made her uncomfortable. She couldn't help looking towards the chair where the girl had sat. 'Sit down,' he said.

'No, thank you.' She wondered why she was reluctant to sit down. 'I'd like to see David, please, if he's at home.'

'He isn't. Can I help?' He wasn't really offering help, it was just a way of saying—what do you want?

He stood, looking at her, a high-powered dominating man, well over six feet tall, and perhaps she was standing too because that might make it easier to move away, to get out. He made her confused and nervous. She didn't want to sit down with him looming over her. She explained, 'This is rather personal. What time are you expecting him back?'

'I'm not. He's in London. He's flying to Canada in the morning.'

So Jenine had been left without a goodbye, David Irving had skulked off, and Sophy said tautly, 'Your brother is a louse.'

She was slightly surprised at her nerve, but it didn't shake Carlton. He asked, 'On what do you base that?' and his calmness spurred her to a blunt reply.

'On a little matter of a pregnancy.'

That got a slight raise of the heavy brows but no change in the tone of voice, when after a moment he asked, 'How long have you known David?'

Sophy hesitated herself; she couldn't see what that had to do with anything, and then she realised what he was thinking and her cheeks and her eyes flamed.

She yelped, 'Not *me*! What is he, the local sex maniac? I'm talking about Jenine Riggs, the girl who works in my shop.

'She thought David was meeting her tonight. She thought they were getting engaged before he went away. She's expecting a baby.'

'And you're representing her?' He sounded as though she was a lawyer or a social worker.

'I am,' she said grimly. 'She's at my house and she's in a bad way, so what are we going to do about it?'

'Go back and tell her I'll be along shortly.' That was reasonable, but it was the curtness of command that riled her. He might employ half the village, but she didn't have to take his orders, and his brother *was* a louse, and if Robert had 'sort of brought him up' as Jenine said, then he should be less composed and more concerned about this affair.

'All right,' she said. 'And don't imagine he'd be doing any favours by marrying her, except for himself. She's too good for him.'

'Miss Brown,' he went ahead of her into the hall to open the front door, 'I suggest that you mind your own business.'

'Don't tell me what to do!' she snapped as she stepped out into the night. Robert Carlton was everything she had reason to dislike in a man, and she was seething with anger against him and against David. What was going to happen now? How was she going to tell Jenine that David had gone and that Robert would be along?

And where was Puppy? He had gone into the house with her, but she hadn't thought about him for the last five minutes. It would be very embarrassing to have to ring the bell again and ask if she could look around for her dog.

But the door was still open and suddenly Puppy bounded out and she rounded on him in irritated relief, 'Come *here*, you idiot!' Hurrying through the trees she said, 'Sorry, I'm a bit tetchy. That man back there reminds me of two other men.'

She went as fast as she could. She couldn't imagine Robert Carlton sliding down the hill and climbing over the fence, he'd be more likely to drive round and he could arrive before she did, which meant that Jenine would be unprepared.

She almost ran through the Stones and went skidding and slithering down the hill, and only slowed up when she was in the garden because she still hadn't worked out how she was going to break the news.

'Sophy, is that you?' Jenine called as she went in through the back door.

'Yes,' she called back. The door between the kitchen and the living room was open and Sophy met Jenine in it.

'Did you see him?' Jenine looked as though she had been crying her eyes out. Her eyelids were shiny and swollen and she had rubbed her face a blotchy pink, washing away all her make-up. She was clutching a handful of damp and crumpled tissues and sniffing as though she had a heavy head cold.

Sophy said, 'Come and sit down'—although she had probably been huddled on the sofa, where Sophy had left her, until this minute—and wondered if she should pour another brandy. Jenine had split most of the first, but maybe it wasn't a good idea to numb her distress for Robert Carlton. Let him see how wretched she was, and certainly she had better be sober for the interview.

'I saw Robert,' said Sophy. 'David's already left.'

Jenine sank shuddering on the sofa again, her face

in her hands and her shoulders heaving. Sophy was feeling helpless. She'd known Jenine less than a month, it was nearly as hard as trying to comfort a stranger. She didn't know what to do with her in this state and she suggested desperately, 'Shall I fetch your sister?' Jenine's sister Beryl lived in the village, but Jenine shook her head and went on sobbing into a cushion.

'Robert's coming down,' said Sophy, and Jenine jerked up as though Sophy was about to open the door to a charging bull.

'Oh no!' She stared wildly around, like somebody seeking escape, and although Sophy was very sorry for her she had to suppress a rising irritation.

'What did you expect?' she demanded. 'You wanted Robert to be told about it, didn't you? You knew you'd have to see him.'

'What did you tell him?'

'What you told me. About the baby, and that David hadn't even said goodbye.'

The doorbell rang; she had only just managed to get here ahead. Robert might have offered to run her back in the car, although she would have hated to ride with him. Jenine went white, only her eyes staying pink and puffy, and Sophy patted her hand. 'He can't eat you,' she soothed. 'There's nothing to be scared about.'

There was a big car parked just outside, and this man standing there. Sophy shoved Puppy behind her and said, 'Come in.'

She took him into the living room where Jenine was white-faced and pink-eyed, and nothing at all like her pretty everyday self. She stared at Robert Carlton, her lips quivering, and he said, 'Good evening' to her, and to Sophy, 'Is there somewhere we can talk in private?'

'In here.'

'Thank you.' He stood by the door obviously waiting for her to leave, and Jenine whispered jerkily,

'Sophy, I'd rather—you stayed.'

Robert Carlton's deep voice imediately turned
down that request. 'It's up to you, of course, how much
you confide in Miss Brown later, but we'll have this
discussion without a third party.'

Jenine looked too scared to raise her voice, and
Sophy wished with all her heart that she could have
found the strength to stand her ground and say, 'This
is my house, Jenine wants me here and I'm staying.'

But even more than her father—far more than her
father—he had this air of absolute authority. He
looked at her and it was as though she was pushed out
of the room. She stumbled past him into the little hall,
and he closed the door almost before she was through
it.

She was ashamed of herself. He had no right to close
her door or order her out of her living room. With no
one else around he could bully Jenine as much as he
liked, and just as soon as Sophy had her breath back
she was going back in.

'I've decided to stay,' she'd tell him. 'After all, this is
my house, and why are you so anxious not to have a
witness?'

She was breathless, running all the way back from
the house on top of the hill, and when you are tense
you do breathe shallowly, and this was an extremely
tense situation. Three deep relaxing breaths and she
would turn that door knob.

She breathed deeply once, then the door opened and
Robert Carlton said grimly, 'Would you mind moving
away from this door?'

All her breath came out in a furious gasp, leaving

her none, so that she squeaked instead of shrieking indignation, 'Are you suggesting I listen at doors?'

'Possibly,' he said. 'You look in through windows,' and under his scrutiny she knew that she was scarlet-cheeked and looking guilty as sin.

He shut the door for a second time and left her gasping. How did he know? He'd had his back to her and she could have sworn the girl was only looking at him. But the girl must have seen her, and Puppy must have left pawmarks in the flower bed under the window, and Robert Carlton probably knew that she walked her dog on the hill most nights.

Did he imagine she made a habit of spying through his windows? 'Miss Brown,' he had said, 'I suggest you mind your own business.' She certainly had enough business of her own to mind. She hadn't the remotest interest in what was happening in his house, and she would be delighted to hand over Jenine's problem to someone else. Not to him, she wouldn't willingly hand anyone in distress over to him, but to Jenine's sister or father or friend. She got no vicarious thrill from other people's lives, her own was more than enough for her most of the time.

She stood in the hall, quivering with frustration because she couldn't say all this to his face. That would have been undignified and emotional, and there was too much raw emotion on display here tonight without Sophy adding to it.

But she had to release her pent-up fury somehow and she went through the shop into the workroom, and got out a lump of clay and began to pummel it. Puppy watched with interest, caught by the violent energy she was expending.

She wasn't modelling so much as bashing a head together and gouging out features, but it wasn't a bad likeness of Robert Carlton when she'd finished. His friends might not recognise him, but his enemies would: big nose, beetling brows, the furrows scarring the forehead and cutting deep from nose to pugnacious mouth. A glowering, craggy face.

Sophy stood back when she'd finished and said, 'Hello and goodbye,' then bashed it back into a lump of clay and felt better for the exercise.

How long did he think he was going to keep her from her own fireside? She checked her watch and was surprised to find she had probably been here ten minutes or so. Although he could say a lot in ten minutes, especially if Jenine stayed dumbstruck so that he was the only one talking.

She shouldn't have let him order her out of the room. Jenine was in no state to argue her rights. She ought to go straight back in there, and in another five minutes or so she would.

Meanwhile she went into the shop, opening the door into the hall so that she would see if he left— because she thought him capable of leaving without bothering to look for her to tell her he was through with her living room—and began to rearrange some of the shelves.

She was on the little two-steps-high ladder, propping plates up against the wall of the top shelf, when he came into the hall. He saw her and paused in the doorway. 'Thank you,' he said. 'By the way, I used your telephone.'

'Be my guest,' she said shortly. The way he'd used her house he might have owned it.

He looked straight at her, that hard penetrating look that sent a shiver like trickling ice water down her spine. 'I don't think so,' he said, then he went and she heard the front door close and the car move away.

When her father had left a room he had still seemed to be around for a little while. Even after he died she had known that the house would never be entirely free of his imprint and influence, that was one of the reasons she had sold up and moved away. The houses and the rooms and the places she had known with Stewart might be 'haunted' by him, and now Robert Carlton had invaded her cosy little sitting room and she had let him take over.

She might have defended her hearth. She might have told him to drop dead and set the dog on him. Except that Puppy was everybody's friend and she had invited him to come in.

Anyhow, she wasn't getting involved in this any further. She was minding her own business, she wasn't asking any questions. But when she saw Jenine, sitting pale and quiet, pity and fellow-feeling welled up in her, because she knew that beaten look. Men like Robert Carlton drained the spirit out of you. She had seen herself looking that way before now.

She offered, 'Shall I make a cup of tea?'

'Yes, please.'

She put on the kettle and got out the cups and there was silence until, just as the kettle was boiling, Jenine said quietly, 'I don't like to ask, but could you manage without me for a few days?'

Sophy's resolution to ask no questions shattered; she had to ask, 'Has he persuaded you to get rid of the baby?'

'I'm just going away to think about things.'

She would have plenty to think about, but she didn't look capable of reasoning rationally, and Sophy made up her mind. 'I'm getting your sister round here.

Or somebody. You need your family behind you.'

'I don't need anyone.' But she did, and Sophy said firmly,

'You're not going off like this, so where does she live?'

She knew where Jenine lived with her father. If it came to it she would go round there and ask for the sister's address, and Jenine said with a little sigh, 'She's on the phone, four seven three,' giving the information slowly and grudgingly.

The voice that answered Sophy was a young woman. Yes, she said, she was Beryl Manders.

'I'm Sophy Brown,' said Sophy. 'From The Potter's Wheel. Jenine's here, could you come round for a minute?'

She thought she might be asked why, but Beryl seemed to understand. She said, 'Of course, he goes tonight, doesn't he? O.K., I'll be along.' So Beryl was prepared for trouble when David Irving left, and that meant that she could know the whole story.

'She's coming,' Sophy told Jenine, who said nothing.

Sophy poured out tea, and a saucerful for Puppy, and they sat sipping silently until the doorbell rang again. Puppy was having an exciting time. It was a rare thing, someone at this door after the shop closed, and now three times in one night. He rushed to answer it, putting his foot in the saucer which was luckily empty by then.

'I'll go,' said Sophy, although Jenine wasn't stirring. She sat, head bowed over her teacup.

Beryl was about twenty-six, with the same fine fair hair as Jenine, but hers was cut short, making her face look plumper. She was plumper, more solid altogether, with none of Jenine's gentle dreamy air.

She came in with a purposeful stride, giving Sophy a

grin and a grimace, then marching up to Jenine. 'Oh, come on now.' The hand on Jenine's shoulder was almost a shake. 'You knew he was going, there's no sense getting yourself into this state.'

'He didn't meet me tonight.'

As Sophy went into the kitchen she heard Beryl say, 'Well, I'm sorry, but I don't blame him if he didn't feel like facing you, saying goodbye and crying all over him.'

It didn't sound as though Jenine would get much sympathy from her sister, which might not be a bad thing. Breezy commonsense support would be fine, except that it could mean Beryl didn't know about the baby. If she had done surely she wouldn't have been so casual.

Sophy waited again. There wasn't much she could do to pass the time in the kitchen, she couldn't even have a cup of tea or lay a breakfast tray, because the teapot and the cups were in the next room, so she went out into the garden and looked up at the stars.

It was a beautiful night. When you looked into the great shining vault of the sky, so still and peaceful, you couldn't believe the mess and the muddle mankind was making of life down here. She picked out a few constellations—she used them on some of her mugs, the star signs and the stars, so she'd had to learn them—and then she heard someone coming through the kitchen door, and turned to face Beryl.

'Sorry about this,' said Beryl.

'It's all right. It's a nice night.'

'Yes.' Beryl stood beside Sophy, the light from the kitchen door and window behind her, her face in shadow, and asked, 'Can you manage if she goes off for a few days?'

'Yes, of course.'

'Do you believe she's pregnant?' Beryl demanded abruptly, without any preamble.

'She says she is.' How on earth could Sophy know? She had believed what she was told, and Beryl gave a wry half chuckle.

'Bit of a romancer, is our Jean.'

'Jean?'

'She changed it to Jenine when she left school. I don't think she is. She hasn't had tests or anything.' She was watching Sophy closely and Sophy wondered if Beryl was trying to stop the gossip before it started.

In every way Jenine had been very indiscreet, but if Sophy had been the only one she'd confided in they need not worry about Sophy talking. She said, 'That would make things easier, wouldn't it?'

'Yes,' said Beryl. 'She's making a great song about everything, but she'll get over it. She'll have to, won't she? Because he's not going to spend the next six months mooning over our Jean.'

Beryl seemed a practical woman, and Sophy felt that was right. David Irving would not be pining for the girl he'd left behind. 'A bit of a break might do her good, though,' Beryl went on. 'She's been a bit run down, and she's a bit low, so if you could give her a few days off——'

'Of course.'

'I'll take her home now, and she'll be back, say a week on Friday.'

'Fine.'

'I work three days a week at the factory. If you liked I could give you a hand in the shop Tuesdays, Thursdays and Saturdays.'

'Thank you,' said Sophy. 'Where shall I say she is if anyone asks me?'

'Blackpool,' said Beryl promptly.

'I hope she has a nice holiday,' said Sophy.

She stayed in the garden a little longer. It was too dark to see the Stones or anything but the black rise of the hill, but up there were the trees and the house, and Robert Carlton.

Whether Jenine was romancing or not Carlton was the hard-headed realist with a heart of stone who could shatter any dream, and he had sent David away, that *was* a fact.

Beryl and her husband worked in his works, Jenine and her father lived in one of his houses, to David he was boss as well as brother. He was the big man in Halebridge, with the power to control other people's lives.

'Just keep out of my life,' she said to the darkness up there near the sky. 'Just keep away from me.'

Later she noticed the money by the telephone and wondered who he had phoned. David perhaps, but whoever it was she didn't want to know; she wanted to stop thinking about it.

Next day she served in the shop, and waited till evening before she did any work in the workroom. She missed Jenine, who had been company even at her dreamiest, and she was glad Beryl was coming tomorrow.

Beryl arrived on time, and said she'd never served in a shop before but she'd soon get the hang of it. She probably would too, as soon as Sophy could manage to persuade her it was poor sales psychology to pounce on customers as soon as they stepped over the threshold.

'Let them look around,' Sophy advised. 'You're here to help if they can't find what they want, but people come into a shop like this to see what there is in the first place.' After that Beryl tried not to look too eager, but her instinct was to grab them and sell to them.

The morning mail arrived, as usual, at about half past nine, and included a registered package addressed to Jenine. Letters for Jenine had come here before, as she left home before the post was delivered there, and Sophy handed it over to Beryl.

There were no customers in and after frowning at the writing Beryl began to open it, while Sophy protested, 'I don't think you should be doing that.'

'It's from Mr David,' said Beryl.

'What difference does that make?'

'Posted in London, before he went.' Beryl tapped the postmark. 'Now what's he got to say for himself?' She read out the enclosed note. ' "Sorry I had to leave early, but Robert found something for me to be doing in town before I get my flight. I shall miss you." ' Beryl rolled her eyes at the ceiling. 'Oh yes?' she said. 'And for how long?' She went back to reading. ' "I'm enclosing a small goodbye present. In haste, with love . . ." And what's this?' said Beryl.

The box was the wrong shape for a ring. She opened it and whistled, 'That's cost a pretty penny!'

It was a silver bracelet watch, and any girl would have been delighted with it if she hadn't been hoping for something else.

Sophy said, 'She was expecting a ring.'

'He told her he'd be bringing her a goodbye present,' said Beryl. 'He didn't say a ring.'

'I see.' So it had been wishful thinking. Poor Jenine!

'Of course she isn't getting a ring.' Beryl sounded as though she had no patience with such nonsense. 'Can you see Robert Carlton's brother marrying our Jean?'

Robert Carlton—as though he was the one concerned, not David. 'Robert Carlton wouldn't like that?' asked Sophy, knowing the answer, and Beryl said,

'Not much he wouldn't, no,' putting the watch and the letter into her handbag.

Two women came into the shop and before Beryl could bound forward Sophy grabbed her and said quietly, 'Let them look round.' Beryl had push, but she would have to learn that this was not a hard-sell shop.

Apart from that drawback Sophy liked having her around. She was as different from Jenine as Robert was from David. She was energetic and unimaginative, running a job and a home with a husband and a five-year-old son. She wasted no time on dreams, she had too many practical problems on her mind, but she liked a laugh and she was kind in an unsentimental fashion.

She was fond of her sister. She had had a couple of phone calls from Jenine, she said; the pregnancy had just been Jenine piling on the agony, she wasn't pregnant, but the holiday was doing her health and her nerves good.

Beryl knew by now that Sophy was respecting all the confidences that had been forced on her, and she was grateful. 'You're a good sort,' she said. 'Our Jean's lucky she's working for you.'

It was on one of the days when Beryl wasn't helping that the young man from the crafts shop in Whitby came in for his cat jugs. Sophy was in the shop alone and she smiled as he looked at her. 'Miss Brown?' he said hopefully. 'I'm Giles Galloway.'

He looked like a Giles Galloway, tall and slim, wearing casual country clothes, green check hacking jacket with leather patches at elbows, and green cord trousers. His fairish hair was just long enough to curl over his collar, and he had sensitive regular features. It was a pleasing face. It kept Sophy smiling while she took him through to the workroom to look at the jugs, which he inspected enthusiastically.

'Oh yes,' he said, 'I'm sure I can shift these.' He looked around at mugs and plates and bowls and casseroles, in various stages of production, with the gleaming eyes of an old prospector striking a promising lode.

'Very good stuff,' he pronounced them. 'Miss Palmer said you were one of the most promising young potters she knew.'

That was nice of Audrey, and in no time Sophy was taking orders, and Giles Galloway was telling her about his shop, which carried all kinds of craftware. It was good, meeting someone in the same line of business, with whom you could talk the same language, and Sophy felt the glow of his admiration because he obviously appreciated her as much as her work.

When customers came he stood around and waited, and he was there all afternoon, feeding scraps of information—like the fact that he wasn't married—into their conversation, which grew progressively friendlier and more flirtatious.

It was the brightest afternoon she had had since she came here, and she knew he was going to suggest a get-together after work. When he asked, 'Would you have dinner with me tomorrow night?' she said,

'Thank you, I'd love to.'

She would have invited him to stay on and have a meal with her tonight except that she had work lined up, but she would look forward to tomorrow. It was time she started getting out in the evenings sometimes, and Giles Galloway was exactly the kind of man whose company she would enjoy.

. She phoned Audrey and said, 'I've just met your cat-jug bloke, isn't he super?'

'Glad you like him.' Audrey laughed. 'We thought he was rather dishy.'

'He's unattached too, and we've got a date for to-morrow night.'

'That's as good as another order for more jugs,' said Audrey gleefully. 'Anything else happening?'

'Not much. My assistant's on holiday.' Sophy was telling nobody the background to that. 'But her sister's helping me out. How about you?'

Talking to Audrey brought back memories of Stewart, of course. He hadn't phoned or written and she was glad he hadn't, although it touched her pride to know that he hadn't cared enough to even try to understand. It was his way or no way.

She still choked with misery when she thought of him, and she daren't even get herself a television set yet because she couldn't risk seeing him pop up on a commercial. But Giles might help to restore her confidence, and tomorrow night she would dress up for the first time since she came here, really glamorise herself.

She was ridiculously excited at the idea of an evening out. She had had a month of unremitting work, and nothing in the way of relaxation except sitting reading by the fire or walking Puppy.

She was varying their walks these days, she had taken him round the village a few times. He was walking to heel quite well, but it did mean putting the lead on him, because even at night the occasional car could shoot through at a dangerous speed. Puppy preferred the freedom of the hill, and so did Sophy.

She enjoyed the climb and then the night breezes on

her face when they reached the top. She liked walking among the Stones, and looking down on the lights. They never went near the house, and they hadn't met anyone else. Until tonight.

Tonight Puppy barked and Sophy wondered if the lunatic fringe was abroad. But it was Robert Carlton who came across and said, 'Good evening,' and she wasn't sure that she wouldn't have preferred meeting a trespasser. She could have beat a fast retreat then, but she could hardly scamper off when he spoke to her.

'Good evening,' she repeated, and her mind went to pieces. She had always known she might meet him when she came up here, it was part of his garden, but she was suddenly tonguetied and rooted to the spot.

There could only have been a few seconds' silence, but it seemed to her that he was never going to break it, and she was never going to get away until someone spoke. They were standing by one of the Stones and she said abruptly and shrilly, 'They look bigger when you're close to them, don't they?'

Well, obviously they did, everything does, what a stupid remark to make! But he said, 'Are you interested in Stone Circles?' and she tried to reply sensibly and civilly.

'I haven't had much to do with any until now, but of course I'm interested in these as I'm practically living in their shadow.'

They seemed all shadow, seven huge hunched shapes. A witch was supposed to have turned them into stone, which seemed a general legend with these small clusters. It was either that or they had danced on a Sunday and been struck by divine retribution.

'The Seven Brothers,' she said softly.

'The story is that there were originally eight.'

'Eight?' She was intrigued, nobody had told her

that. 'What happened to that one?' she asked, and she heard Robert Carlton smile.

It made his deep voice, that she would have described as harsh, sound warm and attractive, and it made her look at him in astonishment.

'He followed the witch, but whether he caught her or not isn't on record.'

'Seeing what happened to his brothers,' she said, 'I hope for his sake he didn't,' and he chuckled, and she smiled too and turned to call to Puppy.

As Puppy came from the fringe of trees she said, 'It is all right me bringing him up here, isn't it? He only went as far as the house the first day.'

'Ah yes.' He was still smiling, so she might as well clear up that misunderstanding now that she had a chance.

'I'm sorry I looked in through your window,' she said. 'I don't make a habit of minding other people's business. I really do have enough problems of my own.'

'And what problems do you have?'

Puppy was beside her, waiting to be petted for answering her summons so promptly, and she stroked his head. 'Just starting a business. I've never done that before.'

'What did you do before you came here?'

'I worked for someone else. In their pottery.'

'You didn't like it?'

'I liked it very much,' she said emphatically, remembering how good Audrey had always been to her, 'but I wanted my own shop.'

'Well,' he said, 'if you should need any help you know where to find me. Goodnight.'

Sophy said, 'Goodnight, and thank you,' and she was almost home before she realised what had just occurred. She had come across Robert Carlton in a disarmingly amiable mood. Of course he could be amiable. Beryl and her husband, who worked for him, seemed to like him, and David had said he was a brother in a million. Of course he had charm, and that offer of advice if she wanted it was probably genuine.

But the last thing she wanted was his interference in any shape or form. 'You know where to find me,' he'd said, but she wouldn't go to him to save her business. She wouldn't go to him to save her life. She had learned her lesson, she was finished and done with men like him.

CHAPTER FOUR

SOPHY intended washing her hair tonight, making up her mind what to wear tomorrow, and thinking about Giles. That was what she had planned, and when she got back from her walk with Puppy she brought out her black velvet skirt and an emerald green silk blouse, shampooed her hair and sat by the fire blow-drying it and listening to the radio.

Meeting Giles was a tremendous stroke of luck—not just for the business but for Sophy. Her first night here, when she had been feeling a little lost and lonely and had promised herself she would meet a nice man before long, she had been hoping for someone like Giles. She had almost dreamed him up, gentle and kind and nice looking, proof that life could come up with good things as well as bad, and she hoped that Jenine wouldn't be too unhappy when she returned, the day after tomorrow.

Remembering Jenine made her think of Robert Carlton, not only on the hillside just now, but in this room last week, standing by that door. She looked across and she 'saw' him, with his aura of strength and power that was almost touchable.

It was infuriating, because he ousted Giles so completely that she had a hard time remembering what Giles looked like until she concentrated fiercely. And that wasn't much use for a dreamy relaxing half hour.

She glared into space, at the spot where Robert Carlton had stood, fixing his forceful personality on her mind and memory; then she exclaimed 'Scat!' and

Puppy jumped up, head and tail swishing, looking for the cat.

'It's all right,' Sophy soothed him, 'it's all in the mind. My mind, not yours.'

Next morning Beryl said, 'I like your hair.' Sophy had washed and set her hair herself since she came here, but last night she had tried out a new style, smoothly waving back from her face, which would be fine unless the night turned damp.

She told Beryl, 'I've got a date tonight. The man I was making the jugs for collected them yesterday, and he asked me out to dinner.'

Beryl's eyes lit up. 'Oooh, where are you going?'

'I don't know.'

'Well, if he asks you, you say Franco's. It's an Italian restaurant in New Halebridge and the food's very good. Jim took me there for my birthday.'

A customer came into the shop and Sophy went back into the workroom to carry on with Giles' order of some marbled earthenware dishes. An hour or so later she was gently shaking one of the dishes to get the effect she wanted, when Beryl came in with mugs of steaming coffee.

'Ready for a break?' asked Beryl.

'Thanks.'

'We've been quite busy.'

'Good.' Sophy took her hands away from the dish and picked up the coffee.

'Tourists, all of them,' said Beryl. 'Except Mrs Tewson. She bought a casserole, one of the big ones.'

Robert Carlton's housekeeper shopped at the grocer's next door but one, an upright woman usually wearing a neat navy blue coat and hurrying. 'I hope they have no trouble with it,' said Sophy. 'I didn't tell you, I met the man himself last night while I was out walking the dog. He was almost human.'

'Why shouldn't he be?' Beryl sounded puzzled, and Sophy explained,

'The other times I met him he seemed about as human as the Stones up there.'

'He's all right, so long as you don't get on the wrong side of him.' It seemed that Beryl bore him no malice, although she might have done for Jenine's sake, and Sophy said ruefully,

'I seem to be dogged by men like that.'

'Men like Mr Carlton?' Beryl couldn't believe it, and it wasn't entirely true. Sophy's father and Stewart had been small-time dictators compared with Carlton, although they were all tarred with the same brush.

'Men that are all right so long as they're giving the orders,' said Sophy, and Beryl laughed.

'I've got two at home, and one's only five years old. Mind you'—it was funny to her, she didn't really know what she was talking about—'they don't get away with it with me.'

'Some do,' said Sophy quietly. 'With some it's a way of life,' and while Beryl was considering that she asked, 'Do you think Robert Carlton stopped David marrying Jenine?'

'If he wanted to marry her,' which Beryl thought unlikely, going by her voice. 'He's always been one for the girls, has Mr David. But if he did I suppose Mr Carlton might have stopped it.'

'And would you say that was right? Dictating what other people do with their lives?'

'Depends, doesn't it?' Beryl seemed prepared to argue. 'If it wasn't for him it wouldn't be much of a life for most of us round here. He made this place, and New Halebridge. There was hardly any work here until he started the factory.'

So Robert Carlton owned Halebridge Agricultural Equipment by his own efforts, not because it had been handed down to him. 'What did the Carltons do before that?' Sophy asked.

'They were the landowners, weren't they?' said Beryl. 'He still owns the land, but he took up engineering and he started the works.'

This was Beryl's last day as Jenine's stand-in at The Potter's Wheel. 'Any time,' she told Sophy, as she said goodbye at the end of the day. 'If the business ever does well enough for you to take on a part-timer I'd like to come back.'

She wasn't bullying the customers any more, and if business ever did improve to that extent Sophy wouldn't hesitate to offer her a job.

'You come round any evening you're fed up,' offered Beryl. 'And I'll be looking in.' She patted Puppy. 'That dog's still growing,' was her parting shot.

Sophy had just shut the shop and gone through into the house when the phone rang in the living room. She hurried to answer it, hoping it wouldn't be Giles to say he couldn't see her tonight after all. Things did happen like that, unavoidable hitches, but it would have been quite a disappointment.

'Sophy?' said Giles. 'All set for tonight?'

'I am that. I'm looking forward to it.'

'So am I. I wondered if there was anywhere in particular you'd like to go.'

She was about to explain that as this was her first outing since her arrival in Halebridge she had no favourites. But it was nice to be asked to choose, her preferences hadn't counted with Stewart, so she said, 'What about Franco's in New Halebridge? Someone told me it was good.'

'It is,' said Giles. 'I'll ring and see if I can book.'

She walked Puppy round the village, a climb up the hill tonight would have ruined her hair-style, which was still sleek so far; and then she started to get ready for her date.

It was luxury, putting on the silk blouse and the velvet skirt, doing the little make-up tricks that emphasised the deep blue of her eyes and the high cheekbones under the smooth skin. She touched silver with the lightest fingertip dab in the centre of her eyelids, outlined her lips and glossed them red and luscious.

Then she applied her best perfume. She hadn't used that since she came here, she had almost forgotten how seductive it was. She breathed in ecstatically, then offered a wrist to Puppy. 'Get that!' she smiled. 'Doesn't that knock you out?'

He licked it and she said, 'That wasn't quite what I meant.'

She had about twenty minutes to spare before she was expecting Giles, and she went around making sure that all doors and windows were shut and secure. She hadn't heard of any break-ins round here, but it was better to be safe, so she checked, then stood for a minute or two at the kitchen window, looking out towards the hill.

Robert Carlton was the sort of man who would live on a hill, somewhere with a vantage view over all the other houses. Sophy wondered if he was up there now, and she wondered again about the redhaired girl she had seen in his home.

'One of Robert's girls,' Jenine had said. 'There's safety in numbers.'

David was a one for the girls, Beryl had said. So were both brothers womanisers, or were both sisters prejudiced? David Irving looked like a lad for the girls, but Robert Carlton emphatically did not. He was attractive to women, no doubt, some women, most women, but he did not look like a chaser.

If the redhead was typical his taste was expensive, downright exotic. Considering that Sophy had only seen her for a matter of seconds she could recall her very clearly: the halo of flame-red hair, the pale oval of her face, the flowing dress in kingfisher blue. She would be tall, and when she moved her figure would have a model girl's grace.

Just thinking about her made Sophy feel almost dowdy and she moved away from the window, shrugging her shoulders impatiently. Why was she comparing herself with Robert Carlton's girl? There was no comparison. So long as she suited Giles, and he suited her, that was all she needed to worry about tonight.

Giles thought she looked marvellous. He said so as soon as he saw her. He stepped into her little hall and said, 'You look marvellous!' as though she had been transformed. And she had a little, from the girl in jeans and sweater with the curly dark hair and sketchy daytime make-up.

He was wearing a lightish jacket and shirt, darkish tie and trousers. He wasn't transformed, but he was quite elegant, and she thought—this is going to be a lovely evening, the first of a lot of lovely evenings.

'I got a table for eight o'clock at Franco's,' he told her. 'We were lucky, there'd been a cancellation.'

'Of course we're lucky,' said Sophy. 'Or we wouldn't have met each other.'

Giles laughed, 'You're right there.' His car was outside, as he settled into the driving seat beside her he said, 'And you smell as good as you look.'

'Thank you.' She snuggled down in her own seat. 'This is my first outing since I came here. It's been all work up to now. I'm looking forward to seeing the bright lights of New Halebridge.'

After Halebridge the lights were bright, although she had been joking. The road that linked the village with the small town was wide and well used, but it was a country road, edged by hedgerows, fields and hills. There were no lights, except for the occasional farm, until New Halebridge came into sight, and New Halebridge was bigger, busier and brighter than Halebridge.

The entrance to the town was dominated by the factory, stretching over several acres, with high gates, closed now, although lights showed here and there in various windows.

The town had grown with the factory, in the last fourteen years, but there were no high-rise buildings, and none of the deadly boxlike uniformity of most new towns.

The houses were built in Yorkshire stone. Terraced, semi-detached and detached, they all looked solid and substantial, good homes with character and roots; and the square in the centre of the town was of a size to take a market. There was a market here on Fridays, tomorrow. Beryl had told Sophy she did most of her shopping during her Friday lunch hour from the factory.

The shops were closed, but the windows were lit and they looked inviting. This seemed a flourishing little town. Looking around the square, as Giles drove round making for the restaurant, Sophy decided that she might have done better trying to get a shop here than in Halebridge. As well as trade being better she would have been away from the hill and Robert Carlton.

She asked, 'Is there a crafts shop?'

'I think the post office has a pottery department.'

I must look them up, she thought, and see if they'd like to sell some of mine.

Inside, Franco's was whitewashed walls, tables set in arched alcoves, lamps swinging from the rafters, and a perpetual flare of flambéed this-and-that being ignited on a central trolley. The tables were full and the waiters were busy.

Sophy read the menu very carefully, savouring the description of each dish as though she was tasting them all. She chose veal on skewers with cheese and Parma ham, served on rice, topped with parsley, and with a green side salad.

It was delicious. She was enjoying the different tastes and textures and listening to Giles telling her about the kind of music he liked. As this was a first date they had plenty of comparing and discovering to do, and she was nodding her agreement that Nana Mouskouri had a lovely voice, and vaguely watching a waiter cross to a table opposite.

Then she almost choked. There were two men at the table, and one of them was Robert Carlton. She felt outraged, as though he was shadowing her and had followed her here, which was ridiculous, of course. She turned her head quickly although he wasn't looking her way. He probably hadn't spotted her, and if he had he wouldn't be interested.

They seemed to be talking business. She tried to give Giles all her attention, but she couldn't sit with her eyes glued on him, as Jenine had with David that Sunday they came to Sophy's to tea. And there was a limit to inspecting the food on your plate. She had to look around from time to time, and the table *was* opposite.

Robert Carlton was hard to miss. He was big, physically, compulsively dominating. He was wearing a dark suit, and against the white wall his shoulders seemed broader than ever. The man with him looked like an American, and several times Sophy caught herself studying them so closely that she could hardly hear what Giles was saying.

She got away with it. Giles didn't notice. He thought he had all her attention, but she felt as though she was being tugged forward in her chair, while she strained to see from under lowered lids, and to hear.

Robert Carlton was no concern of hers. It was Giles for whom she had made herself beautiful—well, as beautiful as possible, and yet she couldn't relax because of the man sitting over there. She was sure he hadn't seen her but, even when she was looking at Giles, she could see him eating his meal, refilling the wine glasses, talking, listening.

It would be confidential, they wouldn't be raising their voices, so of course she couldn't hear them. But beyond the general babble and what Giles was saying—and half the time Giles was practically talking into her ear—she felt she could distinguish the deep murmur of Robert Carlton's voice.

She was becoming obsessed by the man. It was finding him here, on her first night away from the house and the hill, although he probably used the place regularly. His works were just down the road, so this would be a handy place to eat, to take a business colleague.

A waiter appeared the moment he looked for one, Giles wasn't getting anywhere near such prompt service; of course he was known here, and it was ironic that Franco's was her selection, she had chosen the place.

She smiled and joked, and Giles Galloway thought she was one of the brightest and most amusing girls he had met in a long time.

She was trying hard to be good company because she was feeling so on edge that, if she hadn't worked at having a wonderful time, she might be saying, 'Let's get out of here.'

When Robert Carlton and his companion stood up she couldn't repress a sigh of relief, and at the same moment he noticed her.

Sophy saw from his expression that he didn't immediately recognise her, glamorised as she was. She was familiar to him but not instantly known, and even when he smiled and said, 'Good evening,' she wasn't sure he had identified her.

She smiled back and mouthed, 'Hello,' and Giles turned to see. Robert Carlton and his companion didn't have to pass their table, nor did Carlton cross to it. The two men went out, accompanied to the door by the head waiter, and Giles asked, 'Who was that?'

'His name's Carlton, Robert Carlton.'

'*The* Robert Carlton?'

'I suppose so. He lives on the hill behind my house. We've met a time or two.'

'He owns the factory, doesn't he?'

'So they say.' She wasn't going on with this discussion. She'd had more than enough of that man tonight. 'Do you know what age dogs stop growing?' she enquired. Giles didn't, but it did divert the talk from Robert Carlton.

'I had a lovely time,' said Sophy, when the time came to part. Giles had driven her home and kissed her fervently when he said goodbye.

'So did I,' he said. 'Until Saturday.'

Saturday afternoon she was going to see his shop,

and the house and the town where he lived. So it was the beginning, and she was flattered and pleased.

The kiss had caused a pleasant little flutter in her and, except for Robert Carlton having chosen to eat his dinner in the same restaurant, it had been a super evening.

She really must stop being so hung-up on Robert Carlton. Each time she had seen him it had been fairly traumatic—except for tonight, tonight they'd just been eating at separate tables, he hadn't even recognised her—but that was no reason to feel he was hounding her.

Of course he wasn't. She might go for weeks now, months even, without setting eyes on him again, by which time he should be clear out of her system.

But that night she dreamt of him. She couldn't believe it. She woke in darkness, having struggled out of sleep in which she had been held in a man's imprisoning arms. And what made the dream a nightmare was the inescapable fact that the man who was holding her, so close that he was crushing the life out of her, was Robert Carlton.

It wasn't easy to get to sleep again. She was shaking all over, as though her blood was trembling. She couldn't remember ever feeling so churned up. She had to go downstairs and heat a glass of warm milk, and sip it slowly in bed before there was any hope of her sleeping again.

Next morning, when she arrived for work, Jenine looked as though she had been on holiday. There was more colour in her cheeks, and her face seemed a little plumper. She said she'd been to Lytham, and she'd made friends with another couple of girls, student teachers who were on holiday in the same hotel. They had all gone around together.

She told Sophy that while she hung her coat in the hall and Sophy, standing in the doorway between the hall and shop, said, 'Beryl said you weren't pregnant after all.'

'No.' Jenine passed her to get into the shop, avoiding her eyes, looking at the shelves and displays to see what changes had been made. 'No, I wasn't,' she said at last. 'I thought I might have been, but I wasn't.'

Sophy would not have involved herself in this affair if she hadn't been led to believe that Jenine was in desperate straits. She would not have gone looking for David Irving and bringing back Robert Carlton, so she said, 'I'm glad things aren't as bad as they might have been, but from now on I'd rather you talked to Beryl if you want to talk about David. I made rather a fool of myself, didn't I?'

'I'm sorry.' Jenine's eyes brimmed with tears and Sophy reflected that she should have expected that. 'I love David,' said Jenine piteously, 'and Robert wouldn't even let him say goodbye to me.'

The letter had said that Robert had found some last-minute business for David to attend to in London. That could have been deliberate policy on Robert's part, but if David had really wanted to say goodbye to Jenine she had been in the shop all day. If he couldn't manage to call round he could have phoned here, and Sophy was in a mood to point that out; she had had enough of what Beryl called Jenine's romancing.

But Jenine touched her watch and said, very quietly, 'It wasn't a ring,' and Sophy began to feel sorry for her again. It must hurt to be wondering if you had helped to cheat yourself.

She said, 'It's a beautiful watch. Well, now, if

you're all right in here I'll get back into the workroom. It's nice having you back.'

That got a little smile from Jenine, and Sophy worked with the workroom door open into the shop so that Jenine could wander in and out. She was subdued, but as the day went on she talked about her holiday, and didn't say another word about David, so Sophy had hopes that her depression would eventually lift.

Sophy was needing a few more days to complete her order for Giles, and she had to keep the shop stocked. She was making teapots today, which would be finished in a honey glaze, and all morning she threw pots on the wheel, measuring them with calipers for lid size, and then making lid and spout for each. The handles came later.

She was always content while she was working, and today she had more reason than ever for feeling pleased with life. Last night with Giles had been good and tomorrow she was seeing him again.

She said nothing about Giles to Jenine, of course, that would have been rubbing in the pain of David's loss, but it was a nice warm glow to brighten the day.

Just before closing time they had a visit from Beryl, who came to see how Jenine had got through her first day back at work. She brought Stevie, her five-year-old. Stevie was blonde and solidly built like his mother, with a wide grin that showed gaps where his teeth were missing. His grandmother—Jim's mother—looked after him between school turning out and Beryl getting home from work, and this was the first time Sophy had met him.

While Beryl was satisfying herself that Jenine wasn't still 'mooning', and that Jenine and Dad were coming to Beryl's for Sunday dinner, Sophy made friends with

Stevie. He was a friendly small boy, and she chose a mug for him that was waiting for firing and gave it a happy gappy smile like his and wrote 'Stevie's mug' on it, and promised him he could collect it next week ...

Puppy was determined he was going up the hill to-night. When Sophy stood up to take him for his evening walk he made for the back door. He didn't much care for his lead and going harnessed round the village, and she was happy enough to climb the hill.

She preferred it too. She was lucky, having the hill on her back doorstep, and the Stones had become old friends, although there was always that feeling of spookiness about them. It would always be a strange and exciting place.

She was half way round the horseshoe formation when she saw Robert Carlton. He must have been waiting here. He must have seen her and Puppy scramble up on to the plateau, and he had stood waiting. He said, 'Miss Brown, we can't go on meeting like this,' and laughter bubbled up in her.

'Hello,' she said.

'Hello, and how are you?'

'Very well, thank you.'

'Can I offer you a drink?'

Her voice sounded rather high-pitched. 'In the house?'

'Hardly here.'

Not unless he was carrying a hip flask or a Thermos flask. 'Why not?' she heard herself say. 'Thank you.'

She would like to see inside the house, not through a window, and not when she was so worked up about poor 'pregnant' Jenine that she couldn't see anything but Robert Carlton.

They walked towards the house, through the trees, not talking. Sophy couldn't think of anything that needed to be said and the man said nothing. It was quiet up here, but the silence seemed right, not strained, a natural silence, just the sounds of the night and Puppy snuffling along.

Robert Carlton sometimes walked beside her, sometimes a step ahead. He moved so quietly that she could have been alone, if she had not been so conscious of him.

As they cornered the house, making for the front door, she turned back and called, 'Puppy!'

'Puppy?' Robert Carlton echoed.

She explained, 'That was the name he answered to when I bought him just after I came here. I thought he was fully grown, but he's still shooting up.'

Puppy came at a fast trot and as Robert Carlton opened the front door Sophy grabbed the dog. The hall looked full of treasures, there was a vase over there on a black carved pedestal that could be priceless. 'Is there somewhere I can put him?' she asked rather breathlessly, hanging on to his curly coat. 'He is clumsy—I suppose it comes of getting bigger by the day.'

She must have looked absurd, grimly clutching Puppy, a clown of a dog, and Robert Carlton laughed. 'Not an ideal animal for a china shop.'

'Anything that gets broken in my home I can make again,' she panted, 'but I wouldn't like to try to replace that.' She meant the vase, and he said, still chuckling,

'Perhaps the kitchen.'

She kept her grip, guiding Puppy through the hall and down a corridor until Robert Carlton opened a door into a room where Mrs Tewson and another woman were watching television. 'We're putting this fellow into the kitchen,' he told them. 'Do you have a bone or anything to occupy him?'

Mrs Tewson, and the other one who was probably Miss Harris, jumped up, and Sophy said hastily, 'He's quite friendly. He's only a puppy.'

Miss Harris stayed where she was while Mrs Tewson came slowly forward. 'What breed is he?' asked Mrs Tewson.

'His mother was a collie.' Sophy's lips twitched, recalling the farmer's wife telling her what she was telling them now. 'The rest of the litter were ever such pretty little dogs.'

'And you picked *him*?' Miss Harris thought that was an astonishing thing to do.

'Not exactly,' said Sophy. 'He was all that was left.' And now she couldn't imagine being without him. 'But I wouldn't swop him,' she said. 'I got a lot for my money.'

Puppy grinned at her and they left him in the kitchen, with Mrs Tewson who was going through the pantry to see what she could spare for Puppy's supper.

When they came into the hall again Sophy stood looking at the Chinese vase: porcelain so thin it was almost transparent, a splash of golden paint that was a flight of strange birds flying into a distance of azure and turquoise.

She pressed the palms of her hands together, and her finger tips against her lips. She hardly dared breathe near it and she couldn't take her eyes off it. When she spoke it was in a whisper, thinking aloud. 'If you had one thing as perfect as this it should be enough to keep you content for the rest of your life.'

'It should,' shrugged Robert Carlton. 'Can I take your coat?' and she slipped her coat from her shoulders as he moved towards her.

He put the coat on a chair and opened the sitting room door. There would be bigger rooms in this house, but this was obviously a favourite. There was a slight untidiness about it, newspapers on a table, an open bureau. But it was a gracious room with pale green walls, and a burgundy red Persian carpet.

One picture, a lush pastoral scene of a bygone age, could be a genuine Constable, and there was a painting in an oval frame of a lady in a white muslin dress, hair piled high and escaping in tendrils.

Sophy looked from the painting to Robert Carlton. 'Is it——' she began.

'Yes,' he said, before she could finish. 'A Romney.'

'I was going to ask if she was a relation.'

'My great-grandfather's great-grandmother. Unfortunately there's no resemblance.'

The painted face was flawlessly lovely, the lips curved in a secret beguiling smile, and Sophy said, 'She looks a stylish lady.'

'I believe she was.' He drew forward a chair for her, the chair in which the redhaired girl had sat, and she thought—you may not look like your ancestress, but you have style. It may come of owning all this, of being successful in almost anything you choose to do. She said,

'Jenine came back today.'

'How was she?'

'Not pregnant.'

'No.' That seemed no surprise to him, and she wondered if he had known that before Jenine went away. She asked for a Martini with bitter lemon when he asked what she drank, and he brought her glass and sat opposite with a whisky glass beside him.

With Giles last night it had been a simple matter of talking about the things they liked and disliked, that had been getting to know each other, although most of the time she hadn't been listening to Giles. But, with Robert Carlton, when they'd finished talking about Jenine and David, what on earth would she say?

She asked, 'Did you send David away to stop him seeing her?'

'Why do you ask that?'

'I think you might.'

'I might.' He spoke without hurry, but without hesitation and without making any attempt to justify himself, and Sophy demanded indignantly,

'By what right?'

'You've met David?'

'Once. Jenine brought him to tea at my house.'

'Would you have said they were suited or serious?'

It wasn't a fair question; she couldn't read minds, she could only give a superficial opinion. Jenine had seemed very serious, but Beryl, who must know her much better than Sophy could, hadn't acted as though her sister's heart was broken. The last time she was here Sophy had been blazing with anger, now everything had cooled down. She said, 'I think it's serious for Jenine. I don't know about him. I'd be doubtful about him.'

'So would I,' said Robert Carlton drily. 'And I need him in Canada.'

That almost answered her question, although the work was probably the priority. David had been despatched half across the world because that was where Robert had wanted him to be. It had been a business decision in the first place, and Jenine was even less important than she imagined.

'Did he want to go?' Sophy was prepared to hear that he did, but Robert shrugged,

'I didn't ask.'

'You do push people around, don't you?' She wasn't sure she could get this drink down, she wasn't sure she wouldn't choke on it.

He smiled. Her mind stayed cold and aloof, she hated men who shoved others around, but his smile was physically warming. It relaxed her, in spite of herself, like the glow of a fire on a winter's night. 'They can always push back,' he said.

'Can they?' She was half smiling herself. 'You don't look like a pushover to me.'

Not mentally nor physically. 'Not as a general rule,' he admitted. Not ever, she thought, except perhaps by a redhaired girl who had sat in this chair. She wondered how far he let the redhaired girl push him, or cajole him, whether he was putty in her hands, and thought not.

'You're not married?' he asked, out of the blue.

'No.'

'Who was the man with you last night?'

'A friend,' she said.

'An old friend?'

'A very new friend. He's got a shop and I'm supplying him with some of my work.'

'A business arrangement?'

'So far.' The questioning had been so smooth that her answers had come automatically, but she suddenly realised how personal this was and said, 'Mr Carlton, might I suggest that you mind your own business?'

'That sounds familiar, Miss Brown.' He leaned back in his chair, as though they could sit comfortably here for hours, which of course they couldn't. She must be going soon. 'Sophy Brown,' he said. 'Sophy. Yes, I think we're on first name terms by now.'

Something in the way he said her name seemed to touch a nerve inside her. There was no tenderness in it, it was not said caressingly, just spoken in that deep voice, but her flesh stirred as though her body answered.

She said quickly and lightly, 'I'm not sure. Robert Carlton comes easily enough, that's what Jenine calls you. Her sister Beryl calls you Mr Carlton. I don't know about Robert.'

'You'll get used to it,' he said.

Robert, she thought; and she was used to it as though she had used it a hundred times.

He went on, 'About this other matter, your affairs being none of my business. How long have you been here? Five to six weeks?'

She nodded. About that. 'I doubt if I saw the couple who had the pottery before you more than three times in five years,' he went on. 'But you seem to be cropping up all the time. Familiar, I might say, with the most intimate details of my family life. It's beginning to look as though we have an affinity with each other.'

Sophy gave a little gurgle of laughter. 'A *what*?'

'Put it this way, if things are going on at this rate we'd do better agreeing.'

'Agreeing on what?'

'On friendly relations.' He spoke slowly. There was nothing hurried about him, as though he always knew exactly what he was doing so time was on his side. He had a mind that had brought him power and control, and he saw himself and Sophy coming together. As friends, and then what? What kind of lover would he be? Tender or brutal?

Sophy had been sipping her drink in nervous little gulps. She swallowed hard on that thought, amazed at how naturally it had slipped into her head, turning her head away to stare at the mirror that hung over the mantelpiece facing the window, and frowning.

'Yes,' said Robert, 'that was how I saw you at the window.'

As a pale face peering, and then Puppy's footprints in the flower bed. She wondered if he had told the redhaired girl that someone was looking in on them, gone in a flash, and if she could ask now who the girl was.

But she couldn't without admitting her curiosity. 'And decided I listened at doors,' she said.

'That wasn't in your mind?'

'I was trying to find the courage to come back into the room.' Then she had made that clay head to work off her indignation and pummelled it shapeless, and a giggle escaped her that was less amusement than tension.

He was waiting for her to explain the giggle and she wondered if it would sound funny or stupid when she said, 'I did a model head of you in clay while I was waiting. Just to flatten it because there didn't seem much chance of flattening you.'

She had never expected to tell him that. But she had never expected to tell him anything, nor to be sitting here with him, with this strange feeling inside her, like pain, like hunger, a queer aching emptiness.

'A clay figure?' he said, acting impressed. 'You're not the witch of the Stones, are you?' and she grinned.

'I didn't stick pins into it, I flattened it, and you didn't get any reaction, did you? You didn't suddenly feel flatter?'

'Not noticeably. Was it a good likeness?'

'Not very. I was in a hurry.'

Working from memory and fury, but not a bad likeness. Sophy had captured the strength as though he was stone like the Stones, instead of warm flesh and blood, hard bone and sinew.

She looked at his mouth. In her nightmare last night, when he was holding her, she was almost sure now that his mouth was on hers. It was a sensual mouth for all its hardness, and she could remember the feel of it from her dream, and she was staring at him, and she mustn't stare like that.

She said, 'I'd like to model you. A head—a Roman emperor.'

'Turning thumbs down at the arena?' He wasn't taking that suggestion seriously. 'Life or death,' he said. 'Now that would be exerting undue influence.'

Her mind said he could do it very well, that men like him had that kind of influence, but part of her wasn't hating him. Her hands wanted to reach out and touch him.

There was a small white marble figurine on the table beside his glass, poised in dance or flight, in flowing draperies. She asked, 'Is that Roman?'

'Greek,' he said, and picked it up. 'It's been here since the days when young men went on the Grand Tour and came back with things like this.'

It was broken here and there, some of the robe had gone, and an arm. Sophy looked at it in his hands and saw how he held it, as though the feel of it gave him pleasure, and she breathed deeply as though she herself was under his touch.

If she had been she would have wanted him. Terribly.

'I must be going,' she said. 'Thank you for the drink.' She stood up because she had to go, because if she should let herself become physically involved with Robert Carlton that was what it would be. Terrible.

CHAPTER FIVE

WHEN she was back in her own home Sophy flopped down in a chair limp as a rag doll, feeling as though she had just had a narrow escape. There was no doubt that she was finding Robert Carlton attractive, and even less doubt that he was the last man under whose spell she would willingly fall.

She supposed this was an infatuation, a crush. With Stewart she had looked across the room at that party and thought—he's handsome; and he had smiled and she had thought—*yes*, wanting to like him.

She didn't like Robert Carlton, and yet she could develop a longing for him. Her body could. Not her mind. Not the reasoning reasonable side of her.

Any relationship with him would be entirely sexual and ultimately destructive, and no, thank you, she could do without that kind of involvement. She was seeing Giles tomorrow, and Giles was the kind of man she needed. They had things in common, work, tastes in lots of things, from food to music. She could work up a worthwhile relationship with Giles.

All the way to Whitby, as she drove along in her car, she was telling herself—this is marvellous, all afternoon, all evening free. Jenine had always had Saturday afternoons off, but until today Sophy had kept the shop open. Today she had closed and given herself a holiday to go and see Giles, and she was determined to enjoy every minute of it.

Her delight was slightly forced, rather as it had been in the restaurant. She kept reminding herself how lucky she was, and when she reached Whitby she parked and went down to the harbour, to see the small fishing boats and look across at the lighthouses, and breathe in the smell of the sea.

It was lovely, and now she was going to seek out Giles' shop and see Giles. She was looking forward to seeing him, of course, but she wasn't exactly thrilled to death. If she had been she would have driven straight to his address instead of taking a look at the sea first.

He had drawn her a map and now she turned away from the jetty and began to follow instructions. Suppose she had been going to meet Robert and where the cross was on this piece of paper was where she would find him, then her heart would have been beating fast. She knew it would. The thought of him stirred her dangerously, whereas she could think of Giles and feel no more thrill than the sight of the sea had given her just now.

She found Giles' shop with no trouble, climbing the hill to the town and the shopping centre, mingling with the holidaymakers. It was a Victorian building that looked like an old family business, which it was; a high-class crafts shop, with some exquisite silver jewellery in the window.

She went in; a customer was signing a cheque at a table, while several others drifted around. Everything looked very expensive and most of the exhibits looked fragile, porcelain and cut glass. Pottery was upstairs according to a notice at the bottom of the stairs, and it was only when Giles said 'Hello' that she realised she had been looking for her cat jugs rather than for him.

She turned a beaming smile on him. 'Hello,' she whispered back. It was not a shop for loud voices—at least not down here. Maybe upstairs in the pottery department the atmosphere would be lighter.

Giles took her elbow and led her upstairs and she said, 'You've got a very classy place.'

'Yes,' he agreed.

The pottery was selected too. It was gratifying to see her own ware here, and she would have wandered round the shelves inspecting the competition if Giles hadn't said, 'This way,' taking her through the department and through a door at the far end.

The door led into a flat, a sitting room furnished in a relaxed modern style. He had told her he had an apartment here, although he lived most of the time in his parents' home a little way along the coast, and this looked comfortable, he did himself well.

'A drink?' he suggested.

'I'd love a cup of tea.'

He took her in his arms and kissed her, and Sophy wished she could feel more, although she kissed him back and when he let her go he was smiling. 'A cup of tea,' he said. 'Coming right up.'

He had a meal waiting when they returned from a walk round the town, cold, pâtés and salad, and they talked as they ate. The more Sophy saw of him the more she liked him. They were agreeing about everything, it was nice, and she was glad that her cat jugs had brought them together.

After the meal they sat on a settee, with subdued stereo music playing, and Giles twirled the tendrils of her hair around his forefinger, the sea had brought out its natural exuberance, and told her that she certainly was a lovely-looking girl.

'Thank you,' she said.

'Do you think you could love me?' asked Giles softly, his pale grey eyes anxious, although he was smiling. She shook her head and he sounded disappointed.

'You mean you couldn't?'

'I mean I don't know you well enough to know that.' She wanted to go on as they were for a good while yet, she wasn't rushing into anything.

'Is there somebody else?' he asked her, and she shook her head again, and thought of Robert.

'There was,' she said, 'but we said goodbye when I left London.' That was Stewart. Robert had no place in her life nor her thoughts, and she wished she could stop thinking of him. 'How about you?' she enquired.

'You know how it is. One or two, nothing serious.' Giles looked in his late twenties or early thirties. He said earnestly, 'I want to be serious. I want a girl like you to take home to meet my folk tomorrow.'

She was flattered, but she wasn't prepared to be introduced to anyone—much less to Giles' parents—as his girl, so she said, 'I can't manage tomorrow, and I'm too busy these days to handle a serious affair. I'm only in the market for friends for a while. Any use?'

That was how they parted, as friends, and Sophy promised to phone some time the following week. She was wary of another fixed date now that she knew that Giles was looking for a wife. Although he hadn't proposed he had stressed that and, although she would phone and meet him again, she must take care not to give him any wrong ideas.

She couldn't come to a serious understanding so soon, with a man she had only just met, no matter how nice he seemed to be. Some day she might find that she could love Giles, some day, but first she meant to make a success of her business, and enjoy her freedom.

Next morning she did the household cleaning. This was a usual Sunday morning chore, in fact she had no particular plans for today, she had just been excusing herself from being taken to meet Giles' family. Not that she didn't want to meet his family, if the invitation had been a casual one she would have been all for it; it was the serious note that scared her.

She wrote a few letters too. Nothing to Stewart, she'd heard nothing from Stewart. If she had done she would have dropped him a line, but that was over and she was glad. She took Puppy on the lead to the post office. He tugged at times, but on the whole walked well enough, and there was a dampness in the air, bringing the scent of the moors, as exhilarating as the sea breezes of yesterday afternoon.

Sophy was feeling restless. The prospect of going back into the house and finding some more jobs, or even going in the workroom and making a few more pots, didn't appeal to her.

Puppy could do with a good long walk, and so could she. She had been here for over a month and she had never taken a walk over the dales.

When you stood on the hill of the Stones, looking away from the village, undulating hills and valleys stretched out before you, ranging from pale green-grey to jet black, a landscape like another planet, reaching on to infinity.

That was what she would do this afternoon, take a long walk. The weather was quite good, the sun was out, although there were clouds scudding across the sky, and she'd get all this lovely fresh air into her lungs and clear her head of little problems and bothers.

Giles could be a little problem. She didn't want to hurt his pride because anyone could see that he was sensitive, and she did like him. She would have liked him to be here now, to walk across the dales with her. As it was she must settle for Puppy.

She was hunting in the bottom of her wardrobe for her boots when there was a knock on the front door, and she went to the window of the empty bedroom, that faced the street, to look down.

Robert Carlton's car was parked outside her house. She was reluctant to answer the door, but if she didn't it would seem that she was scared of the man. Puppy was making a fearful racket, and she came downstairs in her stockinged feet.

At least she was warned, she didn't look taken aback when she opened the door. She said, 'Oh, hello.'

He had to ask, 'May I come in?' before she moved, and although she said,

'Of course,' she moved slowly, backing away and keeping her eyes on him. Puppy stopped barking and started tail wagging, and Robert came into the hall, closing the street door.

'What's the matter?' asked Sophy.

'Why should anything be the matter?' He was smiling and she wished she had stopped to put on her shoes. Without heels to lift her an inch or two she felt puny. She could get a crick in her neck, holding her head back to look up at him. If there was nothing the matter what was he doing here? She said,

'Then what have you come for?'

'To fetch you.'

'*Fetch me?*' She always seemed to be squeaking at him. Perhaps it was because his voice was so deep that hers seemed to come out on a constantly astonished note. And she was astonished. 'What do you mean, fetch me?'

'I tried to phone you yesterday,' he explained. 'And a few minutes ago.'

'I was out yesterday and I've just been posting letters.'

'You're back now, and doing nothing in particular, are you?'

Sophy was wearing the clothes in which she had done her chores, jeans and a faded pink and purple striped sweater. Her make-up needed renewing, and anyone could see that she wasn't dressed for visitors or for going anywhere special. Robert said, 'There must be plenty of places round here you haven't seen, then we can find somewhere to eat.'

'No, thank you.' She was going nowhere with him. She said, 'I'm just setting off for a long walk over the dales. I've been promising myself that all weekend.'

If he suggested coming too she would have to agree, but she'd be surprised if his idea of entertainment was a long tramp. That suit wasn't tramping gear. 'You're not going over the dales today,' he said. 'The weather's not right.'

Rays of sunlight slanted down through the little dusty window above the front door, and Sophy said, 'It looks right enough to me.'

She wouldn't gain anything by antagonising him. Or perhaps she would, perhaps it would keep him away. If he had tried to speak to her yesterday, and proposed spending the rest of today with her, he must consider her desirable, and there couldn't be much he wanted that he didn't get.

It was a compliment, but she was frightened at the weakness that was stealing over her. She leaned against the wall, pressing her shoulders hard against it, pushing herself away from him. If he didn't keep away she knew what would happen. The physical attraction was explosive, and she could finish in little pieces.

'Do you know the dales?' he was asking her.

'No.'

'Then keep off them today.'

That was an order, and her already tense body stiffened even more. 'Don't tell me what to do,' she said instinctively, and apologised, 'Sorry, but that's why I'm here, trying to run my own business, because I can't stand people giving me orders.'

'That should ensure your success as a shopkeeper.' He was laughing at her, and she said shortly,

'I'm a potter.' She had to sell her productions, but her happiest time was making them.

'I know,' he said. 'You make clay heads and flatten them.' But she daren't smile, because if she did she could find herself going off with him for the day, and into the night.

She said, 'Yes—well, thank you. Another time, maybe.'

Robert Carlton wasn't used to brush-offs, from women or from life. He didn't accept them. The time was delayed, that was all. He said, 'Of course,' and if he had touched her Sophy might have gone wherever he had taken her.

She had to take her walk over the dales now, and so long as she didn't go too far, and kept landmarks in sight, she would be all right. There were hours of daylight ahead, but she slipped a torch into her pocket and wore a mac although the sun was shining.

When she and Puppy reached the Stones she half expected Robert to step out and stop her. There was no one there, nothing but the eerie aura of the Stones, like eyes on her. She called to Puppy—who had had it impressed on him up to now that the Stones were his boundary mark—and went hurrying down the other side.

She went with a rush, slithering at times as bracken pulled up with the damp soil, exposing grey rock beneath. Clinging to everything she could, turning and twisting as she went, she made her way down faster than she would have liked.

Down here the ground was squelchy, covered in short tufted dark green grass and clumps of moss, and in front of her rose another hill, not quite so high as the hill of the Stones.

Puppy was having a wonderful time, darting in a dozen directions at once, investigating a dozen intriguing scents. He raced on up the hill, which was rocky with little rivulets of water running down, showing glistening rock oozing in black soil.

The track up to the top was fairly steep and slippery, and on the top the wind seemed to have risen suddenly. Sophy hadn't noticed it on the hill of the Stones, but here it was hard and cold, blowing from the north-east straight into her eyes.

She looked back, tempted to turn back, but if she did Robert might see her. The house was visible from here, the trees grew more sparsely than on the Halebridge side. Those long windows must have a magnificent view of the dales, and she wondered if Robert was at a window, if he could spot her and Puppy, the only moving things on the top of this hill.

Puppy's hair was standing on end like a thick fur coat and his eyes were gleaming. This was the life! He hadn't realised it was so splendid over the hill, and Sophy might have trouble when she walked him up to the Stones again at night.

The dales were breathtaking however you viewed them. A feeling of desolation rose in her now, but it was fascinating too as she stared ahead, at ravines and crags, and stretches of moorland with the occasional glint of water picked out by the rays of the sun.

There was a hazy edge on the skyline miles away as though the moors never ended, and not too far, in front of a small hill, was a stretch of water, a pool or a little lake. She would make for that, and when she reached it she would turn back.

The slope down was easier than the climb up, and she strode out, farther and farther from the hill of the Stones, although she had a curious sensation of being watched by them. A shiver touched her spine whenever she stood still. That was the loneliness, of course. She was glad that Puppy was with her. She talked nonsense to him and the going was easy at first, so long as she avoided the rocks, the holes and the boggy patches.

The clouds were thickening and the wind seemed even stronger on the level of the moorlands, but she plodded on. Thre was still plenty of daylight left, and she had set herself the target of the little lake. Puppy was game for another ten miles from the look of him, and she wasn't tired, so why not go on?

It wasn't as easy down here to keep the lake in sight as it had seemed when she'd looked across from higher ground. Hillocks and craggy outcrops obscured her view from time to time, but she made for the hill at whose foot she had seen the lake and she reached it at last.

Not a lake, not that big, but a sizeable pool, looking very cold and deep. Every now and then a cluster of bubbles burst through the water. She thought at first there were fish in here and then realised that underground springs were feeding the pool. She was watching them bubbling up, when the slaty grey surface showed the first plopping of rain.

She hadn't looked at the sky for quite a while, but there was no sign of the sun now. Black clouds had covered it, and rain beat down on her upturned face.

Perhaps it would pass as quickly as it had started. She ran round the pool, Puppy with her, towards a dark opening in the rocks at the foot of the hill where there was shelter, of a sort. They were out of the rain, but it was damp and cold with water running down the sides of the shallow cave.

She *was* cold. She had been warm enough walking, but her light raincoat was inadequate for the sudden drop in temperature. Even her boots seemed to have turned clammy, and her teeth wouldn't stop chattering.

There was no break in the clouds at all, this was no passing shower of rain. It was getting darker every minute and she turned her torch on to her small wrist watch, and gasped in horror at the time. She was a couple of hours out. She had shoved up her sleeve about half an hour ago, and given her watch a quick glance and misread the figures on its tiny face.

She had been out here much longer than she'd realised. There were rain clouds up there, but some of that darkness was night coming on, and unless she could get back to Halebridge she would be spending the night out here, soaked to the skin and chilled to the bone, and terrified out of her mind because this was a terrifying place.

'Puppy, we've got to get home.' She clutched his wet fur. 'Do you know the way?'

He might. If he was a tracker, which she didn't think he was, she thought he was a clown, and she would probably have to get him home.

Huddling here wouldn't help. She kept the torch on, thankful the battery was nearly new, and stepped out of the comparative shelter into the blustery wind and the lashing rain, and staggered as the force of both met her.

All they needed was to be blown into the pool. She got away from that as quickly as she could; Puppy was staying by her now and he hadn't a clue which way he had come.

There should have been a faint glow in the sky from the village, perhaps lights from Robert Carlton's house, but the rain, and a strange patchy mist that was rising out of the ground, blotted them out. Sophy could only see as far as her torch showed her, and when that hit the mist it wasn't far.

The rain stung her eyes and she flinched and kept her head down, so that it soaked her hair and trickled down her neck as she staggered on, wet and miserably uncomfortable, catching her feet in tufts of rough grass, tripping over stones that her torchlight hadn't shown her. Then suddenly, as though someone had turned off a switch, the rain stopped and the wind dropped.

She straightened, thankful to be able to stand upright, and Puppy lifted his ears. A deadly silence had replaced the wind and the rain, but if she shouted there was no one to hear and her voice might come back in ghostly echoes. It was ghostly enough, without providing sound effects. The sky had cleared, early stars had come out, but the mist made weird shapes, turning this into a nightmare world.

She had to keep moving, or the clammy cold would paralyse her, but she went slowly, putting each foot down very carefully, keeping a grip on Puppy because if he did wander off—not that he showed the slightest desire to wander—she might never find him again.

She hoped she was going the right way. It was farther than she'd thought, it had taken longer than she'd realised to reach the pool, and there were rock shafts and fissures scattered around, and she was very near the stage where she might lose her head and really panic.

But she remembered the holes in the ground, and she took a step at a time, trying not to look at the mist, just where her feet were going; then Puppy gave an odd little yelp, and she glanced over her shoulder and saw something rearing up behind her like a huge white beast.

She knew it was only a freak of the mist, but she ran, because that was when her nerve snapped, over bracken and stones and hillocks, her torch flickering wildly in her jerking hand, until her feet slithered away and she landed on her back in a hollow, soggy with water, the marshy earth cushioning her fall.

As her breath came back she began to sob, staring up through the mist to the sky. She had never felt so lonely, so afraid, so wet, cold and miserable, and now she'd probably lost her dog too.

Where was she? How far away were the Seven Brothers, and her home, and a warm fire and something hot to drink? Her panic and her fall had left her dizzy, but if she lay here she would stiffen until she couldn't move, so she dragged herself to her knees.

'Puppy!' she shouted, her sobs dry now, soundless, and Puppy slid over the rim of the hollow, landing almost on top of her. She began to laugh at that, hysterically, then she saw the dark shape looming behind him and the screams came, again and again as she cowered back, her hands covering her face.

But even through her screaming she heard the words, and she knew the voice. Robert Carlton, saying wearily, 'Do shut up. Are you ready to go home?'

She bit off the last scream, her teeth clamped on her quivering lower lip, and stared as though he was a mirage. Then he came down into the hollow, no mirage of the mist, strong and solid and he would get her home.

'All right?' he asked.

'I am now.' He had been right about the weather, she should have listened. 'How did you find me?' she asked.

'I followed you.'

'From the beginning?'

'Yes.'

'I never saw you.' He was wearing a dark leather coat, but she should have seen him in the beginning.

'No,' he said.

'Why?'

'Because you were going to get yourself lost.'

She had behaved stupidly and she was grateful. But he might have offered to walk with her, she wouldn't have been keen on that, but she would have accepted. Or he could have stepped out sooner, instead of keeping out of sight and letting her believe she was alone and scaring her silly.

She muttered, 'I could have broken my neck.' She was still sitting in a heap, and he lifted her unceremoniously to her feet, pointing out,

'But you haven't, and from now on you'll treat the dales with respect.'

'It was a lesson, was it?' He wasn't holding her up, just giving a little support with one hand under an elbow, telling her,

'You're not a woman to take advice, so you have to learn the hard way.'

A glimmer of resentment was creeping into her relief. 'I hope you can find the way home,' she muttered.

'I'm a dalesman,' he shrugged. 'Can you walk?'

Sophy was swaying slightly, but she straightened at that. 'Of course.' She sounded confident, but she could have dropped from weariness. 'I'm a bit stiff and cold,' she said, 'that's all.'

'Come on, then.' He went ahead, as if he could see in the dark, or as if he knew the dales as well by night as by day. She followed very close and Puppy even closer. Neither fancied getting lost again.

'How far is it?' She broke the silence after about ten minutes of trudging, with her legs getting heavier all the time.

'Not far.'

She must have skirted that first hill she had climbed, missed it altogether, because they were suddenly at the foot of the hill of the Stones. That was steep and slippery on this side, she had almost slithered down, but she followed Robert up a track she hadn't noticed before, gritting her teeth for a last effort.

The hours on the dales had taken their toll. She was almost crawling and when, nearing the top of the hill, her ankle turned, she could have wept with pain, although it was nothing. She did cry out, and Robert stopped and retraced the few paces he was ahead.

'I turned my foot,' she told him. 'Nothing's broken. It just hurt when it went over. It's all right.' She put her weight down to prove it, and he took her arm and helped her up the rest of the way.

When they reached the Stones she managed a wan grin. 'I think I know my way from here.'

'You'd better come with me.'

'No.' She wanted to get home. She was almost done for. She just wanted to fall down and fall asleep.

'Yes,' he said and, as she opened her mouth, 'If you say, "Don't tell me what to do" again I'll take you back out there and leave you!'

Sophy couldn't argue. She was exhausted, not so much from physical effort as from stress. Her muscles were still tight knotted although she was safe now.

When he picked her up she jerked protestingly and then went limp, because what else could she do? She couldn't start pummelling him. She closed her eyes, her cheek against the damp leather coat, breathing as he breathed in the dark circle of his arms, not thinking about anything, feeling quiet and safe.

When they reached the house he put her down to take out a key and open the door, but he kept an arm around her, and she went with him into the hall, into the sitting room.

It was warm in here. Robert stirred the fire and sparks and flames leapt upwards and, as her fingers fumbled with the buttons of her mac, he came to her, took off her sodden gloves and rubbed her hands gently. His hands were warm and her skin began to tingle with a singing excitement.

Sophy stood still and he finished unbuttoning her coat, slipped it from her and ran his hands over her shoulders and arms, over the firm young breasts under the damp clinging sweater.

'I'll get you some dry clothes,' he said.

The driving rain had managed to soak her. She wondered now if she could have got down the hill and made her way home, and made a drink and got herself to bed. She went to the fire and peeled off her sweater and let the fire glow sink into her, sitting on a thick white fur rug.

Puppy was doing the same, lying in front of the fire on the white rug, bedraggled and filthy. Sophy felt guilty about that, but too tired to do anything about it, except apologise.

She had better get her boots off. They were in the same state as Puppy, and she began to drag at the left one. They were pull-on knee boots and getting them off was usually a bit of a struggle, but tonight they were extra stubborn. She was weaker than usual and her feet were wetter and when Robert came back, a green velvet robe over his arm, she was still struggling with the first boot.

She stated the obvious. 'I'm having trouble.'

'Hang on to something,' he ordered.

Puppy was the nearest thing, but she got to her feet and sat in a chair while Robert knelt down and tugged at her boot; and she gripped the arms of the chair. If she hadn't she would have been yanked forward, and if her fingers hadn't been clenched she might have stroked his brown hair with the flecks of grey.

She wanted to draw his head to her breast, to feel his lips against her skin. The boot came off, and she said, 'Thank you, I was wondering if I might have to sleep in them.'

'I hope not.' He looked up and smiled at her and she smiled, biting her lip, feeling her cheeks flushing at the thought that must be in the minds of both, that tonight she would be sleeping with him.

'Now this one.' That boot came off too, and he held her wet foot in his hand. 'You should have worn gumboots,' he said.

'Next time I will.' He had. He had taken off his leather coat and changed gumboots for shoes. His trousers looked immaculately well pressed, so he had probably changed those too, but her jeans were wet, and her tights.

'You can't sit around in those,' he said.

'I suppose not.' If she undressed in front of him what followed would be inevitable and she would have invited it. But it *was* inevitable, and that was the naked truth. The zip of her jeans was stiff so that it seemed she was hesitating, and he stood up.

'You could do with a hot drink,' he said.

When he had gone Sophy peeled off her wet clothes quickly. She had a slim smooth beautiful body that she had taken for granted all her life, but tonight this man would see it, and she was glad it was beautiful.

He would touch her, here and here, touch her everywhere and every nerve in her was throbbing for his touch, exploring, releasing, possessing. He wanted her, and she wanted nothing in the world more than to take and be taken by him.

She got into the velvet robe and tied it tightly round her narrow waist, then sat down on the rug in front of the fire again, hands looped over her ankles, her chin on her knees, waiting ...

CHAPTER SIX

Sophy's breath caught in her throat when Robert came back into the room. She looked away from him, at Puppy, flat out in front of the fire, and asked, 'What's Mrs Tewson going to say about that?'

'Nothing,' said Robert. It wasn't Mrs Tewson's white fur rug, but as housekeeper she could complain about a great wet dog sleeping on it. If Mrs Tewson or Miss Harris walked into this room they might have something to say to each other about the girl on the rug, wearing very little except a borrowed housecoat. Or were they too well trained to enter rooms without knocking?

She said, 'Thank you,' as she took the glass of what looked like hot milk, and tasted like hot milk and whisky. She sipped a little and put it down in front of the fire. 'I'll listen to the weather forecast next time,' she promised.

'And that's all you'll listen to?'

She had done with being ordered about, and he was used to giving the orders. They were not compatible spirits, but she ached for his touch. 'I'm not unreasonable,' she said, 'but I don't like being dictated to. What's wrong with that?'

'Nothing.' He stood looking at her, her hair drying in a curling halo, a velvet robe swathing her. She looked at him, in his well-cut suit, the silk shirt and the silk tie, and the handmade shoes.

'You're overdressed,' she said.

He took off his coat and his tie, and sat down beside

her in the fireglow, and she undid the buttons of his shirt so that when he drew her close her face was buried against him. The hairs on his chest tickled her lips and the smell of his skin was more potent than any aftershave.

She felt his fingers on the nape of her neck, then he lifted her hair from her eyes, stroking her face very gently, and slowly, slowly, he began to kiss her.

She had never known that a kiss could be like this. From the moment his lips parted hers it was a sensual swooning delight, an intensity of pleasure she had never experienced before.

When he raised his head she lay smiling, eyes closed. 'I want to look at you,' he said huskily. 'I want to make love to you.'

He had already made love to her. She had been pierced to the heart by a kiss. She touched the velvet robe with languid fingers to open it, and wondered who had worn it before.

The chair that the redhaired girl had sat in was over there, turned towards them. 'Whose is this?' she asked, still holding the robe around her.

'What?' He realised what she meant. 'It's been here a long time,' he said.

'Someone left it behind?' Her smile had changed. She was wakeful now. 'Do you have many ladies staying here?'

'Yes.' She searched his face for a sign of triumph, that might mean he thought she was jealous. 'Most of them with husbands,' he said.

But not all. Of course not all. She asked; 'Who was the girl I saw when I looked through the window?'

'Catherine Gordon.' She was not jealous, but woman-like she was curious.

'Is she married?'

'Not yet.'

Did that mean she was almost married, or so attractive that sooner or later marriage was a certainty? 'She's David's friend,' said Robert.

'Poor Jenine!' That proved David even more unreliable than he had already proved himself, but Robert's expression was still non-committal. 'Are you like David?' asked Sophy.

'No.'

No, he was more dangerous than David Irving could ever be, but lying beside him now she wanted him to lie on her, to stop her questions with his mouth, and shut out everything in a blinding, mind-blowing closeness. She didn't want to say any more, but she said, 'Isn't this like David and Jenine?'

'This is like no one but you and me,' he said.

She said lightly, 'You're seducing me, aren't you?' and he began to laugh, sitting up and shaking his head.

'Perhaps it's you who's doing the enticing?'

'I'm doing nothing.' She struggled into a sitting position, clutching her robe still tighter around her, although she didn't realise she was doing that. 'I'm just sitting here,' she said.

'And looking very much more seductive than I do.'

It sounded like a compliment a man might pay you any time: in a car, across a table, meeting in a street. From wordless passion they had slipped into clichés, and suddenly words were all she had. She said, 'I may look prettier, but you don't need to look pretty, do you? You've had a lot of experience.'

'I wouldn't disappoint you.'

'That I'm sure of.' It wasn't disappointment she feared.

'But you've changed your mind?'

Some might say it was too late, that no man could be expected to stop at this stage, and a woman who had gone so far had surrendered her right of refusal. He could have taken her by force and then by art, and no one would have blamed him, and she would have put up only a token struggle.

But he was deliberately giving her time to think and consider. She still had the power of choice, but once she surrendered entirely to him, physically, the power could be his. When he kissed her she had no longer been mistress of her own body. He had the expertise to set her world on fire, and where would she be then?

She said, 'I think I'd better go home.'

His grin was rueful but amused, as though it was what he expected to hear. 'You wouldn't rather come to bed?' he said, and she smiled. She felt faint with longing for a soft bed in the darkness and him, but she managed to sound flippant and gay.

'Yes, of course, but I think I've had enough excitement for one day.'

'Then I shall take you home,' he said. He wasn't annoyed, he *was* amused. He got up, getting back into his jacket, and Puppy lifted a head, blinking sleepy eyes.

Sophy's clothes were where she had placed them, in a pile on a chair, looking surprisingly neat considering her turbulence of mind at the time. If she left them there what would Mrs Tewson think of that? She said, 'I'd better take my things with me.'

'All right,' said Robert. When he had gone she examined her boots, clogged with mud and revoltingly soggy. Perhaps she could borrow some other shoes till tomorrow. Mrs Tewson was big-boned, but Miss Harris looked nearer Sophy's size.

Robert brought in a holdall and she said, 'I suppose

none of the ladies left their shoes behind?'

♠ 'Not that I noticed.' He was packing her jeans and jumper into the case. He took her keys out of the pocket of her mac and slipped them into his pocket. Then he folded the mac and put that in the bag too.

'I don't relish getting into those boots again until they're dry,' she said.

'The car's outside.' She didn't remember seeing it when they came in, but she had been in his arms, she hadn't looked around. 'Here you are.' He handed her the bag and picked her up as she held it.

She said, 'I can walk,' but he took no notice, and again Sophy relaxed.

He was a strong man, he carried her easily, holdall and all. There was no sound of anyone else in the house, it was very quiet in the hall. She looked up the curving staircase to the lights on the gallery, and the closed doors, and wished he would carry her up to bed.

She didn't want to think or fight, she didn't want to go home, but home she was going or he wouldn't have packed her bag for her. She held it in a dangling hand, the other arm round his neck, and Puppy trotting behind.

The air outside was cold and damp, chilling her face, but the car was near the front door and as soon as she was inside she tucked her toes under her and her hands into the wide sleeves of her robe.

Puppy had been let into the rear seat and she glanced back apprehensively. 'He's going to make an awful mess of your upholstery.'

He was padding around, feet everywhere, but Robert said quietly, 'Lie down, Puppy,' and he did.

'The knack of command,' said Sophy, joking but with an edge to her voice, 'is a wonderful thing.'

The man turned in his seat and looked at her. He

said nothing and she could read nothing in his face, but she felt as though he was seeing her naked. Not just her body but her mind, all her fears and weaknesses. As though he knew her completely and she could hide nothing from him, and there was nowhere she could hide.

Without a word he started the car, and they went down the drive into the road that curved through the village. She tried to think of something to say, but before she could come up with a suitable remark they were slowing down in front of The Potter's Wheel.

Robert got out of the car and opened her front door, putting the holdall inside. Puppy jumped out as Sophy scrambled from her seat, wincing at the cold uneven surface of the cobblestones under her bare feet, but if there were neighbours looking out she would rather Robert didn't carry her into the house. His car must be known and she didn't particularly want to start raging gossip.

She went past him through the open door and he handed her her keys, he was still standing on the pavement, and said, 'Are you asking me in?'

He could have followed her, of course, but when he asked she heard herself say, 'Not tonight, but thanks for everything.'

He had probably saved her life out there on the dales. He had taken her where she was warm and dry and brought her a hot drink—most of which she had left. He had kissed her and shown her what lovemaking between them could be. She wasn't sure whether she was grateful for that, or whether she would have been happier without the pressure of his kiss still burning on her mouth.

'Thank you,' he said, and took her hand. Instinctively she drew back and for a moment his hold tightened, then, quietly and without fuss, he released her. It was when she stood away from him that she felt the real pull and his power over her was agonising. She could have cried out her need to go into his arms.

'Goodnight,' he said, and Sophy stayed where she was, inside her house, until he got into his car and drove away.

She fed Puppy and put a hot water bottle into her bed. She should have been hungry herself, but she wasn't. She was tired. She dragged herself around in the green velvet robe, which was long enough to trail and must have belonged to a taller woman—Robert hadn't even remembered who. The redhead was a friend of David's, he'd said, but she had been with Robert the evening Sophy peered in at them through the window, and very cosy they had looked.

Not that Sophy was jealous. She had no claim on Robert Carlton and wanted none. She wanted an early night, and she would get up early in the morning to wash her hair, she hadn't the strength now.

She left Puppy snoring downstairs and went upstairs, turned out the light and pulled back the curtains and got into bed. The stars were still bright. The clouds hadn't covered them again.

She lay back on her pillow and suddenly she was weeping helplessly, more tears than she would have believed possible, until her hair and her pillow were damp. There was no *reason*. The tears just came, filling her eyes and running down her face, and she let them come because she couldn't stop them. It seemed to her that she cried for a long time, and when there were no tears left she sat up sniffing, and fishing for a tissue from a box on the table by her bed.

What had got into her? What was the matter with her? She picked up the crumpled pillow, shaking it hard, bashing it down again and pounding it with her fists. Just as she had pounded the clay head she had made of Robert, wishing it was him. Why she was hitting out at him now goodness knows.

He had followed her and saved her. She could have been out there still, a sight nearer dead than alive. She buried her face in the pillow. 'Damn you,' she said. 'Why did you bring me home?'

Because he could take her or leave her, that was why. She had wanted him to take her and of course he knew it. But tomorrow would do, or next week or next month.

He knew how she felt and there was no urgency for him. He knew where to find her, even if she never walked up to the Stones again . . .

She woke early and lay for a few minutes exhorting herself to get up and get on with the day. She had to wash her hair, unless she wanted to look like a wild girl, so she did that while she was boiling the kettle, and used the blow-drier while she was drinking her morning cup of tea.

By the time Jenine arrived her hair was silky smooth again, and she had the sleeves of her smock rolled up ready for the next few hours in the pottery.

'Did you enjoy yourself?' Jenine asked. She knew that Sophy had closed midday Saturday to go off on a date.

'Yes, thanks.' Nothing had happened on Saturday that Sophy would have minded telling Jenine about, but Sunday was a different matter. Sophy must have looked flustered because Jenine's eyes opened wider as she waited to hear more.

'Pretty place, Whitby,' said Sophy, glad to see the postman passing the window and several letters falling on the mat.

One letter, from London, told her that Stewart had landed a small part in a TV play. He hadn't written to her, but she suspected he would make sure the news reached her by telling everyone who was likely to be keeping in touch. Good luck to him. By the time the play was televised she would be able to watch him without any pangs of regret.

She could probably see him now and not feel badly, and she enquired, 'Do you rent your TV?'

'Yes.'

'What's the number? I think I'm going to get one.'

She phoned the nearest rental shop and arranged for a set to be delivered, then she got down to work. She was doing some hand painting with a fine-point brush, a rather intricate decoration on a goblet, when Jenine looked in and said, 'Mrs Tewson's here.'

'What does she want?' Sophy was trying to keep a steady hand.

'She's got your boots,' said Jenine, puzzled. 'She says she's brought them back.'

'Oh yes, I'll be in.' Sophy put down the brush and the goblet and went into the shop where Mrs Tewson was standing holding a basket, containing Sophy's boots, cleaned and polished.

'Thank you very much,' said Sophy as Mrs Tewson handed them over. 'You shouldn't have bothered, I could have collected them. You certainly shouldn't have bothered to clean them.'

Mrs Tewson inclined her head with a slight smile, that might have been saying, 'You're welcome,' or possibly, 'Orders are orders.' She must have been told who the boots belonged to and to bring them back. Unless she had seen Sophy last night.

She was giving her a hard look now, and Sophy

knew that she was blushing and that Jenine was staring at her.

When Mrs Tewson had gone Jenine asked, 'How did Mrs Tewson get your boots?'

Sophy was tempted to say, 'They walked up the hill,' or even 'Mind your own business', but either would have been unforgivably rude so she explained, 'I went over the dales yesterday and I met Robert Carlton. I got wet and my boots were filthy, thick with mud. He took me to his house and gave me a drink and then he gave me a lift home, and I left my boots up there.'

If Mrs Tewson had asked for the green velvet robe back then Jenine's hair would have been standing on end. As it was she looked shocked and reproachful. 'You never mentioned it,' she said, as though Sophy's reticence was highly suspect.

It was, of course, and quite deliberate. Sophy had no intention of telling anybody what had happened, what might have happened if Robert had not brought her home. But her cheeks were burning hotter under Jenine's scrutiny and Jenine said,

'It isn't the first time you've met him while you've been walking, is it?' Jenine had no idea just how often Sophy had encountered Robert Carlton, how persistently their paths seemed to cross. 'Why did he ask you in for a drink?' she wanted to know.

'Being neighbourly?' Sophy suggested.

'Is he after you?'

She sounded as though Sophy had been put on a list for assassination, and Sophy grinned weakly. 'It looks like it,' she admitted.

She took her boots into the living room. She had never seen such a polish on them. Mrs Tewson must have worked energetically, or indignantly, and Sophy presumed her reputation was lost. If Mrs Tewson gossiped. No, she thought, nobody on Robert Carlton's staff would risk gossiping about him, but now that Jenine had an inkling of how the land lay it might get talked about.

'Is he after you?' sounded as though someone was following behind, waiting to pounce. Like the great white beast in the fog which could have been a polar bear with claws, or a monstrous phantom that would overwhelm you, covering and suffocating.

I am going crackers, thought Sophy. But her peace of mind was being threatened and it would be more sense to do something practical, rather than wait for Robert to make the next move.

He would phone her, or come for her, she was sure. In his time, sure of himself. Well, he shouldn't have given her a breathing space. Last night she would have stayed, but he had brought her home. Perhaps he hadn't wanted Sophy Brown breakfasting under his roof. He wanted Sophy Brown, he was making no secret of that, but perhaps not quite so openly, so flamboyantly.

Possibly there was someone else—Catherine Gordon perhaps, although he had said she was David's friend —so that he would prefer to conduct an affair with Sophy with discretion.

Except that there would be no affair. Last night's madness would not be repeated.

'Giles,' she said aloud, and looked up his number in her address book in the bureau and rang the shop.

She had to wait a few minutes, during which Jenine came along. 'Do you have any matching saucers to the blue soup bowls?'

'No,' said Sophy, 'but I can make some, if they could come back in two days or leave an address.'

'Yes, all right.' Jenine hovered a moment longer and Sophy said,

'I'm phoning Giles.'

She hadn't talked much about Giles, but she had said that he had a crafts shop and that was where she was going on Saturday afternoon.

'Oh,' said Jenine, 'I wondered if you were talking to Robert Carlton.'

'Why should I be?'

'I don't know. Are you seeing him again?'

'I'm not dating him, if that's what you mean.'

'He's old enough to be your father,' said Jenine shrilly. 'He's old enough to be David's father.'

'At thirty-four?' said Sophy. Both Jenine and Beryl had mentioned that he had been twenty-one and David nine when their mother and David's father were killed.

'Hello,' said Giles. 'Miss Brown is you, isn't it, Sophy?'

'A very ordinary name,' said Sophy.

'For a very extraordinary girl.' She hadn't been fishing for that compliment, but he could hardly say anything else. She said, 'Not really. I rang to say thank you for Saturday.' Jenine was still listening, but after that she went away.

Sophy hadn't intended ringing so soon on Monday morning, and she hoped Giles wouldn't think this meant an eager change of attitude. It was a friend she needed, preferably a man friend to be her alibi when Robert came after her again, as Jenine had put it.

'Sorry,' she would say, 'but one lover at a time is enough for me and I'm already suited, thank you. Yes, I know I lost my head a little after my trek over the dales, but I think I must have been in shock because it was quite out of character, the way I carried on, and I can't thank you enough for getting me home safe and sound and so on.'

Something like that, and she would watch that she didn't put herself at risk again, while she built up an understanding relationship with Giles.

She said now, 'I owe you a meal. I wondered if you'd like to come over some evening this week and I'll feed you.'

He said he would, or if she felt that cooking after a day's work would be a strain there was a nice little pub that did supper snacks, about half way between their homes. He could meet her there, tomorrow night, say?

It sounded pleasant, but she didn't mind cooking, she said, she quite enjoyed it and she didn't do much just for herself. So it was settled that Giles should turn up here tomorrow, any time after half past seven.

After she had replaced the phone she wondered why she had been so insistent. It was nothing to do with her determination not to be bossed. There had been nothing in the least bossy about Giles' suggestion, only consideration for her, but she did owe him a meal and perhaps she was anxious to keep the accounts level. She couldn't be sure how things would develop between them. If she backed out, some time in the future, she didn't want to be in his debt.

That was a defeatist attitude. He was a very nice man, and it should be easy to get very fond of him.

She wasn't going up to the Stones tonight, nor any night for a long time. She took Puppy for his walk during the afternoon, leaving Jenine in charge. It was all one what time he went to Puppy, who wriggled through the slats and was nearly at the top of the hill while Sophy was still clambering over the fence.

She hurried after him, he could be off across the dales again if she didn't stop him, but he was loping from Stone to Stone when she got up there. Sophy stood with her back to the dales, arms folded, hair blowing, until she felt the dog had had enough exercise, then they went home again.

Jenine was being rather tight-lipped. She plainly disapproved of Sophy being even neighbourly with Robert Carlton. She said little, with the expression of a girl who could say a lot. Except when there were customers in the shop the only time there was any lively chatter was when the television was delivered and installed, and Sophy signed a cheque and the rental papers, and the two girls were left with the new toy.

Reception was erratic round here with so many hills, but the picture came good and clear as they went from station to station.

Sophy knew something about the production side of TV, and some of the men and women who appeared on the small screen. Most of Stewart's friends were in entertainment, and she had gone along to watch commercials being shot, and once an episode of a long-running police series, in which he had had a one-off one-line part.

She told Jenine, 'My ex-boy-friend has a part in a TV play in a couple of months' time,' but all Jenine said to that was,

'The only one round here we ever see on telly is Robert Carlton, laying the law down as usual.'

'Look,' said Sophy, 'I'm not crazy about him either. But he's done me no harm, and I can't really see that he's done you any.'

'I wouldn't say that,' Jenine sniffed, and Sophy picked up a mug from the table.

'Smash a pot,' she said. 'You'll feel better for it.'

That made Jenine giggle. She didn't smash the mug,

but she did say, 'Is your friend an actor, then?' and Sophy began talking about showbiz personalities she'd met and Jenine brightened up.

The phone rang late. Sophy was thinking about bed, wondering whether she ought to have made herself some supper. Living alone you didn't bother, but tomorrow she would cook a special meal for Giles, and she had opened a tin of sardines when she'd finished work. They were supposed to be full of protein and she really wasn't hungry.

Preparing Puppy's meals was a regular chore, but usually they didn't eat the same things and she tended to cook for the dog and make do for herself.

It was Robert on the phone, and her mouth went dry. 'Will you come out with me tomorrow night?' he asked.

'No.' She added quickly, 'Thank you,' and explained, 'I have a date.'

'Break it,' he said, and he thought she would, just like that, because he had picked up a phone and called her.

'I can't.'

'The next night, then.'

'I'm working. I really am working. I've got a backlog of orders already.' Between Audrey and Giles and her own shop she had enough orders to keep herself busy, although no one was clamouring for supplies.

'Don't overdo it,' said Robert.

He must realise she was putting him off, it must have been obvious, and she hoped he would accept that.

She took a cookery book to bed with her, to plan what she would cook for Giles, and thought what fun it had been when she had had friends dropping in in the evenings two or three times a week. Not that she wished herself back. She liked it here, but it was lonely compared with all the company she used to have, even if Giles was coming tomorrow.

She dropped the book on the floor at last, and as soon as she let her thoughts ramble she found that she was wondering where they would have gone, and what would have happened to her, if she had agreed to spend tomorrow night with Robert...

She enjoyed cooking the meal. She enjoyed serving it up and she quite enjoyed eating it, sitting at her own table with Giles, the glasses of red wine glowing between them.

Giles talked fluently. The more you knew him the more he talked, but Sophy didn't mind. It meant she could take it easy, relax in her chair and be entertained. She had heard better talkers. Some of his opinions seemed rather immature, but probably so did hers, and when she put forward a point of view he was usually ready to agree.

He knew a lot about pottery, and the other things that were sold in his shop, and they talked about work, but mostly Giles talked about himself. He was thirty next month and it seemed to be bothering him.

'Why?' Sophy enquired.

Because he had looked around and realised that most of the men he had grown up with were married, and felt it was time he found himself a wife.

He was looking at Sophy. He was making something of the fact that Sophy had turned up at the moment of his big decision, and she felt like one of her cat jugs, selected as suitable. 'Don't you feel it's time you settled down?' he asked her solemnly.

If this was a proposal she would want a long time to consider. 'I'm twenty-one,' she said. He seemed to think that thirty was panic stage, although she

couldn't see why a birthday should send one frantic-
ally searching for a partner.

You looked, of course, and if one came along who
was right that was wonderful, and she did like Giles,
who was saying now, 'A lot of women are married at
twenty-one.'

'Some marry at sixteen and some wait till they're
sixty,' she prevaricated.

'But there is nobody else?'

She had told him that at their last meeting. She said,
'No,' looking down as though she was lying and her
eyes might betray her. Then she made herself look
straight at him because she was telling the truth, there
was nobody else, and perhaps if she kept away from
Robert she might one day find her heart hammering
when she looked at Giles.

She said, 'I told you, I'm building up my business.
That's my ambition right now.'

There was no hammering heart tonight. She cleared
the table after Giles had gone and thought—business
is flourishing, and I've just been asked if I'd like to
settle down with an eligible nearly-thirty-year-old.
Things are going great for me. So why do I feel as flat
as ditchwater?

As she moved around Puppy went backwards and
forwards to the back door and she said at last, 'I'll take
you to the end of the road if you like, but you've
finished going up to the Stones out of working hours.'

It wasn't likely that Robert would be walking up
there but, as he had pointed out, they did seem to have
this habit of turning up, facing each other, and she
would be safer keeping off the hill.

Jenine was waiting for the post now. If David intended writing to her the letters should be arriving,
and Sophy wished she had asked him to address them

to her home rather than to the shop. Every morning Jenine watched the letters fall through the letter box if she was at the front of the shop, or came scurrying from wherever she was when she heard them dropping on the mat.

The letter box was in the shop door, and if she was close Jenine watched for an airmail envelope. So far there hadn't been one, and although it was early yet Sophy suspected that David Irving was a lazy letter writer. And that when he did write he wouldn't put the things down on paper that Jenine was waiting to hear.

But this morning Jenine was also waiting to hear about Sophy's date with Giles, and Sophy talked about that at length. She didn't mention marriage, that wouldn't have been tactful, but she showed that she was keen enough on Giles to reassure Jenine that Robert Carlton stood no chance.

That cheered Jenine up, and of course it was absolutely true. Come to that, Giles wasn't the most important thing in Sophy's life either. Like she told him, she was determined to make a success of her business, and she spent the morning carefully filling a packing case with pottery to be delivered to Audrey.

She thought this afternoon she might drive over to New Halebridge with a few specimens and see if the owners of the post office, who had a pottery section, would be interested in displaying her wares.

In the winter there wouldn't be many tourists passing this shop, so her best policy would be supplying others, and there was no better time than the present for filling up an order book.

She closed the workroom door about two o'clock that afternoon, then left Jenine in the shop and told her, 'I'm off to New Halebridge.'

'Oh?' said Jenine with a wealth of meaning.

'To the post office,' said Sophy. 'I was told they sell pottery, I thought they might sell some of mine.'

But as she passed the gates and the buildings of Halebridge Agricultural Equipment she could understand why New Halebridge stood for Robert Carlton in Jenine's mind. It was his town, like the cattle barons in the old Wild West tales. If she managed to get her pots on display in the post office she wondered if he might say, 'This town ain't big enough for both of us,' and tried to giggle and realised she was feeling nervous.

They were nice at the post office. A husband and wife ran it and they looked at the samples she had brought along, and thought that local ware might be a good idea. Halebridge Pottery. Sophy left with an order, and time enough to walk round the small town before the other shops shut.

She had parked her car in the square, as near to the post office as she could get, and she looked across at Franco's and wondered if Robert would be dining there tonight, with a customer, or a date. She really knew very little about him, except that he was the man who gave the orders round here, and every nerve in her cried out for him.

She was nervous because she was in his town, not because they might not have fancied her pots at the post office. She got back into her car and drove away, and when she glimpsed a big dark car in her mirror for one wild moment she thought he was following her.

The car was an American one, nothing like his when she gave it a second look, and she was a complete fool because she would have enjoyed walking round the shops. There wasn't much excitement to be rushing home for.

Jenine was pleased to see the order. 'Aren't you clever?' she said.

'Anyone can do it.' Sophy believed that, but not everyone had her flair. It was inborn, that talent for making everyday things beautiful. 'I could teach you,' she said to Jenine, as she had offered before, and again Jenine shook her head.

Last time it had been because she thought she was getting married, because she thought she was pregnant. This time she looked at her hands, which were soft and white with long polished pearl nails, and said, 'It does ruin your nails, doesn't it?'

Sophy's nails were short, but she had never considered them ruined before. She had slim strong fingers and she didn't bother to hide a grin as she said, 'You would have to file them down, but everything has its price.'

'I don't think so,' said Jenine, putting her hands in her pockets, and Sophy began to think seriously about taking an apprentice. If orders went up. If anyone suitable round here wanted to be a potter. Beryl might, she thought. She would have a word with Beryl.

She went on working after Jenine had gone home, and she would have worked until bedtime if the doorbell hadn't rung. She looked through the shop window as she came through, to go into the hall and answer the house door, and there was no car parked outside. So it wasn't Robert.

But it was. Robert carrying a carrier bag, and at the sight of him she felt faint. Tonight he didn't ask if he might come in, he stepped in as soon as she opened the door and said, 'Are you alone?'

'What?' She ought to say, 'No', but that would be ridiculous. he certainly wasn't going to ravish her. 'Why?' she asked.

'Because there's only enough in here for two, so if you are entertaining he'll have to go.'

He meant that. If he had come last night, while Giles was here, he would have ordered him out, and it was not beyond the bounds of possibility that Giles would have gone. 'We have business to discuss, do you mind?' Robert might have said, and Giles would have left them to it, because Sophy might well have been as speechless as she was now.

Robert went off down the hall, into the living room, Puppy walking with him, tail wagging, while Sophy was still goggling. He had that effect on her, strength and sense seemed to desert her, especially if he came on her unexpectedly.

She took a deep breath, unclenched her clenched fists, and went running after him, demanding, 'What's only enough for two?'

He was in her kitchen, emptying his carrier bag of various packages; one contained easily enough steak for three. She said, 'Are you expecting me to cook that?'

'Of course not.'

'Well then?'

'I'm cooking it. Put that in the next room.' He handed her a bottle of red wine that she nearly dropped, and asked, 'How do you like your steaks?'

'Well done,' she said, and scowled in case he should misinterpret that.

'Settle for medium rare,' he said, 'and it will be on the table in ten minutes.'

As usual she could do nothing, except perhaps go into hysterics and order him out, and she doubted if she had the stamina for hysterics at the moment. She said, 'I don't like steak medium rare, I like it well done,' and when he said,

'All right, twenty minutes,' that was as far as she was getting in standing up for her rights. So she shut the kitchen door and went back to her workroom.

It was no use trying to work any more. She washed her hands and took off her smock, but she wasn't going upstairs to even comb her hair, much less put on any make-up. She would have made another clay head of him, except that he might come in and see it, and she had done that once and it hadn't worked.

Walking in as though he owned the place, talking about seeing off any man he found here as though he owned her. She paced and seethed, and when he opened the workroom door she glared. Robert said, 'Come on, it's ready.'

The table was laid and the steaks smelt good. Just steaks and mushrooms and tomatoes and bread. And the bottle of wine uncorked. Sophy said, 'You might have waited to be asked.'

'How long?' He knew the answer would have been never. She said,

'Did the neighbours see you come in? They probably saw your car on Sunday, so just make sure they see you leave, will you?'

'Does that worry you?'

'No,' she said, honestly.

He held the chair for her to sit and she suddenly wished she had changed. Robert was immaculate as usual. He said, 'Have you eaten?'

'Well, no. I fed the dog.'

Puppy was waiting for more, the smell of the steaks in his nostrils and a smile on his face.

'You don't eat enough,' said Robert. 'You're too thin.'

'This is the way I've always been.' She probably had lost a little weight since she came here, but last night and tonight she was dining heartily. And that was the only similarity between last night and tonight.

Everything else was utterly different, especially Giles' honourable intentions. Giles wanted to marry her. Or somebody. He wanted a wife who would fit into his way of life, and with whom he could settle down.

A wife was the last thing Robert wanted, but her heart hammered every time she looked at him, and although she should have resented him sitting uninvited at her table—even if he had brought his own food—she was filled with happiness.

He didn't talk about himself, he got her talking. She found herself telling him where she was born, how her father had reared her. Not that her father had ruled her life, but when he asked why she left her job as soon as her father died she said, 'To do what I wanted to do.'

'Be a potter?'

'Something like that.'

'You enjoy your work?'

'I love it, and I've been lucky.' She told him a little about Audrey and the pottery in Richmond where she had learned her craft. 'I'm still supplying them,' she said smugly. 'And I got an order in New Halebridge today, the post office. They're going to launch Halebridge Pottery—how does that sound?'

'Fine,' he smiled at her, his eyes speculative. 'You're doing all this yourself, single-handed?'

'Yes.'

'Will you manage it?'

'Of course I will.'

'I'd like to see your order books.'

Her order books were her own concern and no one else's. She said sweetly, 'So long as you show me yours.

I might be able to give you some advice.'

That was a laugh, but he understood that she meant —mind your own business. He said quietly, 'I'm off to Paris on Thursday for three weeks, how about coming with me?'

She would like that, she would love it, but wild horses wouldn't drag her. 'Sorry,' she said, 'there are all these orders waiting.'

'If there weren't would you come?'

'No.'

'Why not?'

Because she was trying to break the hold he had over her, not make herself his captive for ever. She said, 'Because I don't go off with strange men,' and he laughed.

'I'm not that strange.'

There weren't many like him, that was for sure. Sophy said drily, 'You don't take no for an answer, do you?'

He shook his head, so sure of himself that she could have thrown a wineglass in his face. 'This time you'll have to,' she told him. And he would. 'I am not available.'

She remembered the velvet robe upstairs; he must take that back when he went. When she wore that she had been available and he probably thought they could take up where they left off. 'I've been doing some thinking,' her voice was light, 'and I don't think an affair would be a good idea. It would complicate my life.'

'Life is complicated.' He reached for her hand and his touch ran like a shock through her whole body. 'But this might simplify it,' he said.

For the moment nothing would be simpler or easier than for her to say, 'Yes, I'll come to bed, yes, I'll come to Paris.' But from then on his power over her might be unbreakable, and her fingers lay still, his hand closed over them.

She said, 'No, it would not,' and he let her fingers go.

'All right,' he shrugged broad shoulders, as though he was making a minor concession. 'I won't make love to you unless you ask me to.'

'That's very accommodating.' Did he think a time might come when she would go to him and say, 'I love you, love me'?

She didn't love him, this wasn't about love. This was simple chemistry of the flesh and she didn't trust him any more than she trusted herself.

She said, 'I hope you're accommodating enough to go home as soon as we've finished eating.'

'Of course,' he said. 'Will you walk with me as far as the Stones?'

They climbed the hill, Puppy racing ahead, a light breeze blowing. Sophy knew her way to the top of the hill by now, she only needed a little moonlight to keep her surefooted. They climbed without saying much, and when they reached the plateau she said, 'I hope you have a successful trip. It is a business trip?'

He wouldn't have been proposing to take her to Paris on three weeks' holiday, would he? 'Yes,' he said, and of course it would have been business first.

She wondered if he would kiss her goodbye and if he did how she would manage to say goodbye. But he didn't, although he said, 'You won't come with me?'

'No, thank you.' She added cynically, 'But I'm sure you can find someone who will.'

He didn't deny it and the breeze had struck suddenly chill. Sophy said goodbye and called to the dog and began to retrace her steps down the hill.

Halfway down she looked back and Robert hadn't moved. She could see him in the moonlight, the Stones rising behind him. He looked watchful and still, like one of the Stones, but closer.

CHAPTER SEVEN

AT least with Robert gone Sophy could breathe freely for three whole weeks. She could walk up the hill and know she wouldn't meet him, or answer a phone and be fairly certain the voice would not be his.

That was going to take some of the stress out of her life. Perhaps most of the excitement too, but she wasn't admitting that. She told herself she was delighted he was going away. He couldn't go too far nor stop too long for her. By the time he came back she could be free of him, she might even be on the way to falling in love with Giles.

She wasn't all that sure she wanted to fall in love with Giles, but certainly he was more restful to have around than Robert.

And there was work to be done. She wrote to Audrey, 'I've got a one-woman factory going here, and I've even got myself a brand name, Halebridge Pottery. So please will you take some of it when I start selling?' She mentioned that she'd heard about Stewart's TV part and that she'd look out for him, of course. Then she went on to tell Audrey about visiting Giles' shop, and she couldn't resist slipping in, 'By the way, I've had a marriage proposal—I didn't know I was such a fast worker!'

That might shut up the ones who were going to keep her posted about Stewart's life and loves, because she wasn't interested; and it would amuse Audrey and reassure her that Sophy had at least one friend up here who would like to be more than a friend.

It was a pity that Jenine didn't want to learn pottery. Sophy found it hard to understand why she would rather stand around in the shop, waiting for customers, than make things. Even a day spent turning out the same shape over and over again left Sophy with a feeling of satisfaction, because each piece was individual and she had a delight and an enthusiasm in her craft.

But Jenine didn't want to know. She was still waiting for a letter from David, and Sophy's comforting line—about him having a lot to do, settling into a new job in a new country, and the postal services being erratic anyway—was wearing thin.

Then an airmail letter came. Jenine saw it drop through the letter box and fell on it with a glad little cry, and Sophy felt quite guilty when Jenine wailed, 'It's for you!' and almost flung it from her.

Sophy didn't recognise the writing, nor could she think who would be writing to her from Paris. If she had stopped to think she might have come up with Robert's name, but she tore it open right away and the signature was quite a surprise.

As she gasped, 'Oh!' Jenine, who had been looking at her with dull eyes, said apathetically,

'What's up?'

'Nothing.' It was a short letter, he was writing it as night fell, and Sophy, who had never been to Paris, suddenly got a mental picture of the Seine, and the bridges and the little cafés, and experienced a sharp pang of regret as though she had missed out.

Of course she couldn't have gone with him. That would have been lunacy, and of course she would go some time. Not with Robert, but not alone. If he was writing to her it looked as though he was alone. Writing this would only take a few minutes, he could have a lady in waiting and the evening and the night ahead, but somehow it read as though he was alone.

Sophy was biting her lip thoughtfully when Jenine said, as though she had suddenly seen the light, 'Paris!'

'Yes, it's from Robert,' said Sophy. 'He thinks I ought to take an apprentice.'

He did say that. She could have handed the letter over to Jenine, except that Jenine might have read it as a love letter. Robert Carlton's few lines expressed wish-you-were-here, if not in actual words. But he did say that he thought Sophy should be wary of taking on more orders than she could deal with, and that help in the pottery should be considered.

'What's it got to do with him?' Jenine demanded.

It was advice any friend might have given. Sophy had come to the same conclusion herself, but her instincts were strongly against letting Robert influence her in business, or in anything else. She shrugged, and Jenine muttered, 'He isn't taking over in here, is he? If he is you can have my notice.'

'No, he is not,' Sophy snapped. 'Not in any way.'

She was sorry David hadn't written, but she was not going to be treated as though she had done something criminal in receiving a letter from Robert.

It was very likely that Robert had influenced David, Robert was a forceful man, but when it came down to hard facts the real reason David Irving had walked out of Jenine's life was David.

She turned away. If she took on an apprentice right after getting this letter Robert would think he'd given the orders, so she'd leave it for a week or two; there was no hurry. With any encouragement he was going to start keeping an eye on this business.

It was small fry to him, no sweat, but she didn't

want his help. From saying, 'I think you might do this,' he'd soon be saying, 'Do that,' and even if he was right she wanted to earn her own success through her own mistakes.

When she got back into the workroom, carrying the rest of the post still unopened, she found that Jenine was just behind her.

'Yes?' Sophy made the enquiry brisk.

'Don't listen to him,' said Jenine.

'I usually make up my own mind,' said Sophy. Well, she had since she came here and that was how she meant to go on.

'The advice he gave me didn't do me much good.' Jenine glowered, with a wealth of unspoken meaning. 'Although it worked out fine for him. It got things just how he wanted them to be.'

She seemed to be implying that her early story of being pregnant was true, and that she had taken Robert's advice. She wasn't pregnant now, but David wasn't writing, and that was how Robert had wanted things to be.

It seemed a heartless little tale in which no pity had been shown, and Sophy probably never would learn the truth of it, but it increased her determination to keep out of Robert's clutches herself.

She got down to work and she kept at it. She was tired when the day ended so that she almost stumbled up the hill with Puppy, and while he raced around she leaned against one of the Stones and rested.

There should be another Stone somewhere if there were eight of them, she reflected lazily. Or perhaps the eighth man was supposed to have followed the witch a long way, miles away, before he caught up with her and she turned him into stone too.

Sophy felt half way to stone herself, chilled and

numb and tired, and now she would go back and have a bath and an early night. If Robert had been at home she might even have gone along to the house and said, 'This is no business of mine, but I did get involved in it, and I would like to know what happened on that little holiday Jenine took right after David left. What was the advice you gave her that she's still so bitter about?'

Oh lord, she thought, it's a lonely world; and she pulled her cloak around her and called Puppy and went back to her lonely little house.

The airmail letters kept coming. Robert wrote every day, just a few lines, but each time it was like hearing the deep voice breaking into a smile. They brought him so vividly to mind that she was getting no rest from him at all.

Perhaps she should have torn them up, but really there was nothing in them anyone could object to. They weren't love letters. They were just notes, as though each night he thought of something to tell her: something funny, something interesting, a description of a scene, a person, even a recipe.

She thought wryly—as they continued to drop through the letter box—a girl could get used to a man like this. Not in any dull prosaic way, but hooked, so that he was necessary to her because he provided the spice to living.

He knew she must be lonely. She had come here from London and a host of friends, and this was a clever way of keeping his hold on her, tightening it even, when Giles should have had a clear field.

Giles didn't produce any more surprises. He accepted that she was considering his offer of a steady relationship. They met and ate together and she enjoyed his company, but she wasn't instantly happy at the sight of him, and his goodnight kisses only left her longing for Robert.

With Robert a kiss had thrilled and shaken her until she hardly knew what she was doing or where she was. She knew where she was with Giles, in his car in a very uncomfortable position, and she disentangled herself and said, 'Goodnight,' as gently as possible.

A few minutes later they both drove themselves home.

One day Giles came into The Potter's Wheel, to collect some more pottery, and Jenine who had been waiting to see him said, 'He's a bit like David, isn't he?'

Sophy couldn't see the resemblance. David Irving was younger, but he had seemed more sophisticated to her and much more selfish. 'You think so?' she said.

Jenine did. She had had a card from David that morning, a picture postcard, and she was trying to rephrase the wording so that it said something else. What it did say was that this was a great country, and he had spent last weekend in Calgary.

'Anyhow,' added Jenine, as they watched Giles drive away with his supply of pottery in the boot, 'you'd be safer with him than with Robert Carlton.'

'Did you say—like David?' Sophy could have muttered, but she didn't. She murmured, 'I'd be safest of all on my own.'

'Oh, you don't want that.' Jenine sounded as though that *was* a fate worse than death, and Sophy laughed, 'Me and Puppy and my potter's wheel.'

Her potter's wheel was taking up almost all her time. The idea of Halebridge Pottery fired her imagination. Up to now she had put no personal sign on her work, but she began experimenting with identifying marks. Perhaps a squiggle representing one of the Stones, with the signature Halebridge across it, or just an H beside it.

Colours too. Glazes that captured the Dales in all their changing seasons. She enjoyed mixing glazes; Halebridge greens for instance had limitless possibilities.

She was working early and late, alight with new ideas. She would have liked someone to try out the ideas on. Audrey would have been ideal, she was a potter, she understood, and the phone was there, of course, but that wasn't like having someone here in the workroom, who could see what you were trying to create.

Jenine thought everything was lovely. Giles knew what sold, but she was limiting her dates with Giles to one evening a week.

Beryl called in the shop one afternoon, and came into the workroom where Sophy was making bowls on the wheel and stared around her. 'What are you doing?' she asked. 'Have you heard there's going to be a shortage?'

'I've got orders for this lot.'

'Need any help?' Beryl stood watching, while Sophy finished the bowl on the wheel, sponged the inside dry, and cut it free with a double twisted wire.

'Do you want to learn?' said Sophy.

'Yes. Yes, why not?'

Sophy placed the bowl on a shelf of bowls. 'I can do with some help, although it will take a while to train you, of course. Can we say in four weeks? I'm too busy right now, I've got to clear these orders, but I was thinking of taking on an apprentice. I did ask Jenine.'

'I know.' Beryl gave Sophy her exasperated woman-to-woman look. 'She's worried about her hands.' She chuckled at that, then she said, 'I looked in to see if you'd like to come round to supper.'

'Thank you.' She'd like to, but she did have all this work.

'Tomorrow,' said Beryl firmly. She jerked her head towards Puppy. 'He doesn't look as though he's going short of much,' and Sophy grinned,

'He isn't.'

'But you're looking a bit tired.'

'Me?' Sophy put on her brightest face. 'I'm not tired. I'm getting my beauty sleep and I'm feeling fine.'

She was glad that Beryl was coming, she had been going to ask Beryl, and it was only stubbornness on her own part that had stopped her saying, 'How soon can you start?'

There were plenty of ways in which Beryl would have been a help, just talking over the designs for one, but that would mean Robert coming back and finding that Sophy had followed his advice, and then he would go on advising. If she waited a month at least it wouldn't look as though she had jumped smartly to obey orders.

That evening one of Stewart's commercials appeared on TV. He was one of three handsome young men being bowled over by a girl who was walking by, wafting clouds of yet another new perfume. One by one, as the scent hit them, they were supposed to express the realisation that here was the girl of their dreams. And as three seconds were all the cameras gave them each they had to get the message at the speed of light.

Sophy recognised the jingle that led to Stewart's brief appearance, dressed as a window cleaner, and took her first look at him since she had left him standing on the pavement, just over Richmond bridge, and driven away shaking. Now she watched while he was on the screen, and let out her breath when the camera reached number three, the junior executive.

That hadn't hurt at all. Why had she thought it might? He was fantastically good-looking, but in less than two months his power to hurt her, to even touch her, had vanished.

She hadn't been in love with him. She had known that just as soon as she took stock, and realised the price she had to pay for being with him. It wasn't love, so it hadn't lasted. As soon as she broke free she was free, and it would be that way with Robert, only she couldn't pack up and go again.

She had to stay free and stay here, and that was harder. Especially as the letters went on coming, and everybody knew about them; and when she went into shops people asked her, 'When's Mr Carlton coming back?' or sometimes they just looked at her as though she interested them.

She had quite expected Beryl to get his name in this morning, and she knew there was no chance of getting through supper tomorrow without a mention of these airmails.

Sophy hadn't written back, and he would be stopping soon or he'd be home before they arrived. You'd think silence should have had some effect on him. He never suggested she should write, although he had written a hotel address at the top of a couple. She'd told him an affair wasn't on, but everybody in Hale-bridge thought it was; and as she was a newcomer they must think that either she was a fast worker, or she had known Robert Carlton before she came here.

Jenine knew she hadn't, and Beryl. And she wasn't the fast worker, he was. She was the one being pursued.

He was out to gobble her up but she was too tough a morsel.

She had today's letter with the rest of her mail on the table. She pulled it out of the small pile with a forefinger, and began to smile in spite of herself. She would not be gobbled, but all the same part of her was finding this flattering and wondering what would happen next.

One of the things he had done, that Sophy didn't hear about until two weeks later, was call on Audrey on his way through London.

Audrey phoned just as Sophy was about to leave for Beryl's and commented, 'You don't spend much time at home, do you?'

That took Sophy's breath away. Except for one evening out with Giles she had worked until around ten o'clock most nights. She said, 'I'm always here, what are you talking about?'

'Well, I've tried two or three times. Different nights.'

'I could have been walking the dog, I suppose. I was out on Wednesday with Giles—you know, Giles Galloway.'

'I tried on Wednesday.' Audrey sounded surprised and rather disapproving. 'What were you doing with him?'

'Not much,' said Sophy, smiling because it seemed an odd question.

'I shouldn't have thought you'd have had any time for him,' said Audrey. 'Oh, we did like Robert!'

Sophy choked as Audrey went happily on, 'It was a surprise.'

'It must have been. He—called on you, did he?'

'Didn't you know, dear? He was at the television studios, so it was only a mile or two away, and he came to see us because you'd told him such a lot about us.'

Not that much, surely. He must be curious about her past to seek out her last employers. What was he trying to find out? The better to know you the easier to seduce you, was that the idea? Cunning but scarey, she didn't want her secrets handed over.

She asked, 'What did you tell him about me?'

'We talked about you, of course.' Audrey sounded like a fond aunt, which was very near the relationship they had. 'Oh, we *did* like him,' she said again.

'I've noticed that he isn't short on charm,' said Sophy wryly.

'When are you going to marry him?' Audrey sounded as though she was hugging the receiver and when Sophy said,

'I'm not, no question of it,' Audrey's voice came different and startled.

'Why ever not?'

'Bed has been discussed,' said Sophy caustically, 'but not the marriage bed.'

'But you said he'd proposed to you. In your letter.'

Sophy could see where that mistake had been made. 'Not *him*. Giles. Giles is pushing thirty and he thinks he should be getting married. I think his parents think he should too, because he's looking for a nice girl to take home to meet them.'

Audrey was taking a little while to absorb this. 'Besides,' Sophy went on gaily, 'I'm a potter, I could supply the family shop at cost, so I ought to be suitable.'

'You're not serious?' Audrey said then.

'Not really.'

'We thought it had to be Robert,' she sounded disappointed. 'He does seem very fond of you.'

'He fancies me,' said Sophy. 'It's good old lust,' and Audrey laughed, cheering up.

'You're having quite a time up North. Giles Galloway seemed a dishy young man, but Robert——' words failed her.

'Sexier?' Sophy suggested.

'My goodness, yes,' said Audrey. 'But not a man to take for granted. I can't see him letting you play fast and loose.'

'Can't you?' said Sophy. 'I'll let you know how things go on.'

'You do that,' said Audrey, 'and send us some sketches of Halebridge Pottery.'

Sophy had sounded lighthearted talking to Audrey about her two admirers, as though she was having a wonderful time. Giles asking her to marry him, and Robert Carlton—rich and powerful and with all the charm in the world—very fond of her. But when she put down the phone she wasn't smiling.

In three or four days Robert would be in Halebridge again, and when she thought of that the hunger began to build up achingly inside her, as though he was her lover and she couldn't wait to fly back into his arms.

Beryl and her family were very welcoming. Five-year-old Stevie was sitting up, waiting to say 'Hello' before he went to bed. When he did go he took the mug with him, that Sophy had decorated with his name and his gappy grin.

'He takes it everywhere bar school,' said his mother.

They had a comfortable home that Beryl kept shining bright, and Beryl carried a large casserole to the table and proceeded to ladle out healthy helpings. Jim was a quiet man, it was Beryl who did the talking, but he often smiled when he looked at her, and he seemed to be proud of her energy and efficiency.

Beryl was keen to start her 'new job'. Her mother-in-law was more than willing to look after Stevie when he came out of school. Beryl would keep on her steady job at the factory and come in to Sophy one or two days a week.

She was quite excited about it, and Sophy was happy enough to talk to her about making pots. 'Jenine doesn't seem interested,' said Sophy, after supper, wiping plates as Beryl washed them.

'No.' Beryl deposited another dripping dish in the draining rack. 'She's always been a dreamer, she never settles for what she can get.'

'Are we talking about David?'

'He's sent her a card, hasn't he? I don't know what he told her, but not half as much as she makes out I'll bet. She thinks she's living in a fairy tale, she always did, even when she was a kid. You've got to be practical in this life, haven't you?'

Beryl was practical. As she spoke she looked round her little kitchen, at the stripped pine dresser and the matching polka-dot china, and her eyes shone with pride.

Sophy polished a plate slowly and said, 'You're happy?'

'Yes, I am.'

'You're lucky. You got the right man. It doesn't happen so easily for all of us.'

As Sophy spoke she realised what Beryl could be making of that, but Beryl showed surprising tact for once by only saying, 'Yes, I was lucky, with Jim living just up the road.'

The only mention Beryl made of Robert Carlton was when the news came on the TV. Jim had been watching a sports programme, and the girls had been talking quietly, sitting side by side on the settee.

He turned up the sound at the news fanfare and

they all listened for a few minutes, then Beryl said, 'Mr Carlton's on on Wednesday night, isn't he?'

'On what?' asked Sophy.

Beryl gave her a sharp sideways glance. 'Telly. Well, they say at work that he is.' She thought Sophy was being secretive and Sophy said,

'I didn't know.'

Not when he's been writing to you every day? said Beryl's disbelieving expression.

'He didn't mention it,' said Sophy.

She had to watch, of course. Wednesday was not a convenient evening because it had been her regular date with Giles for the last two weeks, they were slipping into a Wednesday routine, but it was early evening.

It came under current affairs, it must have been recorded the day Robert called on Audrey. Sophy was trotting between the kitchen and the living room table when Robert's name was given and she stood still, a tray in her hands.

Seeing him on the screen had the same effect as seeing him in the flesh. Each time it was a little shock that made her heart jerk and her stomach drop, like hitting a pocket of empty air in a plane.

She just stood there. He was opening another factory—this was the first she had heard of that—in Scotland, and that was what they were talking about. He sat relaxed, facing the reporter who was interviewing him, immaculately and expensively dressed, looking like a man who knows what he wants and how to get it.

There had to be risks in business expansion these days, but you knew that he'd expect his money back and more. Difficulties wouldn't worry him. He'd build on them. She couldn't imagine anything bringing him down.

He made her feel tired, just looking and listening, and she shivered and wondered if she could have caught a cold from somewhere. Her walk on the moors in the storm was too long ago to be causing chills, but she would rather have stayed home tonight by the fire than climbed into her car and gone out to meet Giles.

She was wearing a jumper suit, a blouson top and a full skirt in very soft rust-coloured jersey, and she went upstairs again and put a black polo-necked sweater under it, and changed her one-bar shoes for her boots. All the same, she was only warm in patches all evening long.

The pub was popular, especially at this time of year when overnight tourists often filled it, and most nights there was a group singing in the big room.

The group had a rollicking repertoire of country songs, and Giles put an arm around her and they looked a loving pair, with him whispering in her ear. But they weren't. What was between them so far was a friendship without roots.

She couldn't even tell him she wasn't feeling too good, because she would be going home soon anyway and it seemed a pity to be a spoilsport now that he'd come out to meet her. She would have told a real friend, 'I feel washed out,' instead of smiling and pretending to be full of life.

When she got away she wondered how long this could go on. Giles was being patient, but he was hoping for more than holding hands and kissing goodnight in the car park, while Sophy was finding him no more attractive than he had been at first sight. She had liked him at first sight, but she hadn't wanted him passionately. Nor did she now. When Giles' arm was resting along her shoulders she hardly noticed it half the time, but Robert's touch stirred something primitive and instinctive.

If Robert made love to her it would be like food and drink after starvation, bringing incredible delight. But no lasting happiness, and she only hoped she could go on remembering that.

Puppy slept in the back of the car going home. She took him along with her these Wednesday nights, they let dogs into the pub, and although he was big he had enough sense to stay tucked away under Sophy's feet.

She talked to Puppy a lot. As she filled her hot water bottle she asked him, 'Wouldn't it be ghastly if I went down with the 'flu, just when I'm starting to work up my business so that you and I can be rich and famous?'

She was joking about being ill. She couldn't remember ever being ill, but she could remember feeling a whole lot brighter than she did now. Her night was restless and next morning she woke with a headache. Not a blinder, but a throbbing pressure like a tight bandage round her forehead, and for the first time she almost regretted being her own boss.

Before she came here there were others who would have taken over. She could have stayed in bed another hour or two, or even all day. But she had to be up early this morning because a batch of pottery being glost fired would be ready.

Her first Halebridge pottery, and she couldn't wait to take it out of the kiln and gloat over it. It would have been twice the fun if there had been someone else to share the moment with her. When Jenine came in she'd say it was nice, but she said that at every stage about everything.

'Right, Puppy,' said Sophy, 'would you care to be

present at the unveiling of the first genuine Hale-bridge pot?'

Waking with a headache might have warned her that she was in for a bad day. She was feeling sorry for herself before she opened the kiln door, but when she did open it she wept.

At an early stage during the firing the top shelf had collapsed and instead of the neatly placed hard-glazed pottery she had expected to see there was a pile of glued-together wastage.

The loss of several days' work would have been a calamity at any time, but this batch had been special —the first, the Halebridge prototypes. It was like a horrible omen, everything spoiled and ugly. Sophy had wanted to get them on show and on sale by the end of the week, that was why she had been putting in such killing hours, and she *was* feeling rotten.

She shrieked, 'Oh no!' then she burst into tears.

There was nobody to come running. She could have sobbed away for the next two hours, until Jenine was due to arrive, and no one would have offered a hand-kerchief or a shoulder. Puppy looked interested, but apart from him she had the place to herself and the tears dried themselves.

She had to start all over again. Hardly anything could be salvaged from this mess. She could accept the delay in the schedule she had set herself, or she could try to think of it as a challenge. Challenges were supposed to be good for you, if you were determined to be a winner. And she was very determined. Maybe Hale-bridge Pottery would never become a household name, like Halebridge Agricultural Equipment, but it was her brand, her creation.

Although she couldn't hurry the drying and firing processes she could work even harder and longer to make up some of the lost time, and she would. She grabbed Puppy and hugged him. 'Right, partner,' she said, 'back to the wheel.'

She didn't tell Jenine what had happened. There was no sense moaning over spilt milk or spoiled pots, both were a waste of time. Besides, if she did start talking about it she could well burst into tears again.

She cleaned out the kiln—a foul job, getting rid of the dripped glaze—and disposed of the debris. Then she started working in clay.

'You look as if you've got a cold coming on,' commented Jenine, and Sophy sniffed.

'I could have, but if I ignore it it might go away.'

She dosed herself with four-hourly aspirins, masking some of the symptoms, and worked all day and half through the night. She got up early and went on working, and Jenine brought in coffee and asked, 'Is this a rush job?'

'Yes.'

Jenine shook her head; such dedication was beyond her. 'You do like your work, don't you?'

'I'm crazy about it,' said Sophy, through gritted teeth.

'If I were you,' said Jenine, 'I should have an early night, because I think you're overdoing it.'

Any fool knew that, but as soon as she had her replacements she would slow down to a reasonable pace. It was just that she wanted to beat the jinx that had done for her first Halebridge batch.

She couldn't have an early night, but she wouldn't make it too late, and she was boiling the kettle for a cup of tea and a few minutes' break, about ten o'clock that night, when the phone rang.

'I'm home,' said Robert. As he spoke Sophy could

almost feel him standing beside her. 'How are you?' he asked.

'Fine.' That was an automatic answer. She closed her eyes and gripped the phone tightly.

'Will you walk up to the Stones and meet me?'

Her eyes opened wildly at that. 'No.'

'Then I'll come down.'

'*No!*' But he had hung up, he was on his way, and she dropped the phone as though it had become burning hot, and stood dithering. She hadn't expected him, not today, not this time of night. What was he coming down here for? What a sight she must be!

She grabbed a comb and tugged at the tangles in her hair until tears came into her eyes. There was no time to do anything, and between fatigue and confusion her head was swimming.

When she heard the knock on the front door she called, 'Go home!' Then she went slowly out of the living room, down the little corridor and opened the door and said it again, 'Go *home!*'

He stepped in, brushing against her in the confined space. The only light in the hall was from the living room. When he reached the living room he waited, and as she came up slowly he held out both hands.

She didn't take them, so he took her, his fingers pressing the soft flesh of her upper arms. 'Now let's have a look at you,' he said.

She knew how she looked. If she had known he was coming she would have made herself half way attractive. There would have been colour on her lips and cheeks, and the shadows round her eyes would have looked less like bruises. 'God Almighty,' he said at last, 'what have you been doing to yourself?'

She said, 'I think I've got a touch of 'flu.'

'You should be in bed.'

'I'm going to bed.'

It was as though a spring had snapped. Suddenly she felt weaker than water and a hundred years old. If Robert hadn't helped her to a chair she probably couldn't have made it, and yet ten minutes before she had been planning another hour's work before bed.

Her hands were shaking, the shaking was going through her like an ague, even her voice shook. 'I've been working full pitch. I had an accident with a batch I promised, and I'm trying to catch up.'

'And trying to kill yourself, by the looks of you.'

'N-nonsense,' she said feebly.

'Are you eating?'

'Of course.'

He went into the kitchen and came out with her camel cloak, that hung with her mac on the hook behind the door. He draped it over her shoulders, fastening the clasp at her throat, and when he lifted her to her feet it was as though her body had given up.

She didn't want to lean on him, but at the same time she wanted to be looked after. For a little while, until she was herself again.

His car was outside. Puppy jumped into the back and Sophy slumped in the passenger seat. She didn't know where he was taking her. To the doctor's? Somewhere to eat? She was frightened by the weakness and the nausea that were suddenly threatening to overcome her. She wasn't used to being ill, she was never ill, but if she had been told now that she had contracted bubonic plague she wouldn't have been all that surprised.

The car stopped at the Carlton residence, and clinging to Robert's arm Sophy tottered in. He called to Mrs Tewson as they went into the hall, and the housekeeper came hurrying.

'I've got a patient for you here,' said Robert.

'I'm so sorry,' said Sophy mistily, 'I don't know what I'm doing here, but I do feel peculiar.'

Mrs Tewson touched her forehead and made a knowing face. 'That's well up. Shall I get her to bed?'

'Of course,' said Robert.

It was either bed or curl up down here on the carpet. Sophy was hearing hardly anything now but buzzing noises. She wasn't sure whether she was going to faint or die, but one way or the other darkness was going to swallow her. She said, 'Thank you very much,' and closed her eyes.

When she opened them she was in bed. She hadn't met the local doctor before, but as the man standing by was enquiring how she felt she gathered that was who he was. 'Horrible,' she said, and he smiled, taking her temperature.

'When did this come on?' he asked as he checked the thermometer.

'It's been creeping up on me for a day or two.'

'Run down, are you? Tired?'

'Tired, yes.'

They gave her pills to swallow and something in a glass and she went to sleep again. She couldn't remember ever sleeping so soundly, she must have been worn out. Only one dream surfaced next morning and that was of the girl whom she had seen through the window, David's friend, standing beside her, wearing the green velvet robe and with her red hair falling loose, and asking, 'What are you doing in Robert's bed?'

She remembered that right away, as soon as she woke. It was a question she would do well to ask herself. This wasn't Robert's room, it was very likely a guest room with its matching sprigged lilac wallpaper and counterpane, and crisp white net hangings on the white fourposter bed. But it was in Robert's house and she should be in her own bed in her own home.

Her watch was on the bedside table and the time was almost eleven o'clock. She lifted the bedclothes, which felt very heavy although they were only a sheet and a duvet, and sat on the side of the bed, her toes in the thick lilac carpet.

But when she tried to stand she couldn't. She was incredibly weak and the nausea was still there. She had to crawl between the sheets and wait until someone came.

She didn't have long to wait. Miss Harris looked in, silently as though she had done this several times before, and said, 'Ah, you're awake,' when Sophy's wide eyes met hers. 'You needed the rest,' said Miss Harris.

Sophy tried to sit up. 'What's the matter with me?'

'You've got a virus.' Miss Harris smiled and promised, 'You'll be all right in a day or two. I'll bring your breakfast up.'

'I'm not hungry.'

'You must eat. That's why you've caught this, because you're run down.'

'I should be going home,' Sophy protested.

'Mr Robert's arranged everything.'

'That's very kind of him, but——' But Miss Harris had gone, and Sophy sank back. She could hardly argue her case for independence when she couldn't stand, let alone go home and look after herself.

The food was served on a tray covered with a white napkin. The china was eggshell and each time a nosegay vase had a different arrangement of tiny flowers.

They fed her with tempting dishes; sometimes Miss Harris brought up the tray, sometimes Mrs Tewson, and each time Sophy apologised and each time she was reassured that there was nothing to apologise for.

She must be making extra work, but Robert had said there were often visitors, so perhaps it was part and parcel of their routine. When she was strong enough to move she would buy presents, if she could find out what they would like. She was very grateful to them, two strangers nursing her.

It wouldn't happen again. She would never let herself get into this state again. She asked Mrs Tewson, 'What's happening to my dog?'

'He's here, he's all right,' Mrs Tewson assured her.

'And my shop?'

'Jenine Riggs,' faint distaste flitted over Mrs Tewson's face, 'and Beryl Manders are looking after it.' Beryl! That was a relief!

'Don't worry about anything,' said Mrs Tewson. 'Mr Robert said to impress on you there's nothing to worry about.'

'You're very kind,' Sophy said. 'And this is all a great imposition.'

Beryl turned up during the afternoon, her eyes darting round the room. As soon as Mrs Tewson left them she said, 'Smashing place, isn't it?'

'Four star at least,' Sophy grinned weakly.

'How are you feeling?'

'Pretty groggy. Thank you for stepping in with the shop.'

'Oh, that's all right.' Beryl was carrying a carrier bag, a small overnight bag, and several magazines, as though she was hospital visiting, as though she expected Sophy to be here some time. She put the magazines down on the table and the bags beside the bed and Sophy said,

'Thank you, but——'

'I'm staying on full time until you're quite fit again,'

Beryl announced. 'I'm getting my pay from the works, so you don't need to worry about a thing.' So Mrs Tewson had said. 'Mr Carlton's taken the books to check your orders,' Beryl added as though that should take a load off Sophy's mind. 'Everything's in hand.'

In Robert's hands—the last place she wanted them to be. Beryl peered at her. 'Sophy? Are you all right?'

'Just overwhelmed,' said Sophy.

'He's taking a big interest in you.' Beryl didn't know what to make of this. Mr Carlton wasn't like Mr David, there was no roving eye about him. Everyone accepted that he was a confirmed bachelor. The women he went around with were the ones whose pictures you saw in magazines, but he hadn't married any of them and she couldn't see his interest in Sophy lasting. 'It's very nice of him,' she said.

'Nice be blowed,' said Sophy bluntly. 'Robert's no knight in shining armour. He's a man on the make, and he's altogether too overwhelming for me. You couldn't call your soul your own with him.'

She was amused to see Beryl flush, and realised how much Beryl respected Robert Carlton. Stolid down-to-earth Beryl was shocked at Sophy's plain speaking.

'I brought your nightdress and dressing gown and things in there,' Beryl said, and began to turn out the carrier bag, producing a bunch of grapes and some home-made biscuits. While Sophy was thanking her she was saying, 'I didn't think you were looking too good, but I didn't realise you were ill.'

'It was my own fault,' Sophy admitted. 'I struck a hitch in production and I tried to work extra hard, and I was already working too hard, so I picked up this beastly virus.'

'Now you know,' said Beryl, and Sophy smiled.

'I know I can't go without food. By the way, how's Jenine taking this?'

Beryl's grin crept back. 'She thinks he kidnapped you.'

'He nearly did. I more or less flaked out as he arrived.'

She couldn't help that. She had reached the end of her tether. If Robert hadn't come she would have had to crawl to bed at that stage. It wasn't a question of giving up because he was there and she knew he would look after her. She didn't want him looking after her, and as soon as she saw him she would start making arrangements to go home again.

But when she did see him it wasn't that simple. There was a knock on the door and she called, 'Come in,' and Puppy bounded through, spotting her and making for the bed, gathering himself for a spring and landing on her legs. He seemed to weigh a ton. Sophy gasped 'Get off, you fool!' and Robert laughed.

'You wouldn't be talking to me?'

She stroked Puppy's head and shoved him off the bed, smiling, and Robert asked, 'How are you?'

'Better.' She wriggled higher on her pillows, sitting up was more dignified. She was feeling better than last night, but when she got home she must take things easy for a couple of days. 'This is a super nursing home,' she said, 'but I think I should be discharging myself.'

He drew up a chair to the bed, sat down, and looked at her closely. 'The question is—are you safe to be loose? You don't seem to have any idea how to look after yourself.'

She had been an idiot, overworking and under-feeding herself, but all she needed for full recovery was a short rest and sensible eating in future. The trouble was that when he was near all she wanted was for him to hold her and comfort her, and tell her he would make love to her as soon as her head stopped aching.

She was in Robert's bed and she wasn't going to get any stronger here. She was going to get weaker. Well, but weaker.

She babbled, 'Of course I can look after myself. I didn't realise you could get physically low so quickly. I've skimped on meals. If I wasn't hungry I haven't bothered, but if you don't eat your appetite gets less, doesn't it?'

'Don't ever do that again,' he said, putting an arm around her and holding her to him, his lips on the warm hollow of her throat under the fall of her hair, then on the softness of her breasts where the night-gown had slipped away.

She felt the restraint in the gentle hold, but her own resistance was being replaced by a wild urgency. As soon as Robert touched her she wanted him, that was the power he had, and every moment of closeness was making it harder to drag herself away.

But she did, jerking back, sideways, feeling the pain of separation tear through her. 'Please don't,' she whispered.

He tucked the sheet up under her chin, perhaps solicitously, perhaps mocking her modesty. 'Anything you need?' he asked.

'You're doing too much.' That had a double meaning and he grinned ruefully,

'So it seems.'

'I mean, taking charge.' She had to get this said. 'I'm grateful, everybody here has been so kind, but I don't want taking over. My business, for instance, I don't want anyone telling me what to do about that.'

'All right.' He was sitting back, still smiling at her, humouring her, and she went on desperately,

'But you can't help it, can you? You've got to be in charge. People who get near men like you aren't allowed to live their own lives.'

'No?'

'Take David and Jenine,' she blurted. 'Did you advise her to have an abortion?'

'Self-interest is rather overriding with David,' he said. 'I've no doubt he told the girl whatever she'd believe, but he didn't leave her pregnant.'

'That was considerate of him,' she said with a flash of contempt.

'Reprehensible,' he said drily, 'but not untypical.'

She had to agree, and some of the things David told Jenine were probably true. It was no lie that Robert had not wanted him to marry Jenine.

She said impulsively, 'He told her you were against young marriages because you were let down years ago, by the girl you nearly married.'

She had wondered about that girl, and it was a stab that might get under his skin. She wanted to shake his composure but, apart from a raised eyebrow, he showed nothing. He looked surprised, slightly amused.

'Were you?' she persisted, and he said,

'I never nearly married anyone.'

He was honest. He wasn't blaming anyone for his cynicism. He wasn't married because he didn't want to be, and she heard herself say, 'Not even Catherine Gordon? I had a weird dream last night that she came in here and stood there and asked me what I thought I was doing in your bed.'

That dream had niggled at her mind. She had

almost mentioned it to Mrs Tewson or Miss Harris, but she knew now why she had waited to tell Robert about it.

'Not even Catherine,' he said, and she knew somehow—not from his face nor his voice, but somehow she sensed it—that she hadn't dreamed.

Catherine Gordon had been here last night. She had been in the house the night Robert came home, waiting for him, of course, and he had gone to Sophy because, for a while, Sophy was the girl he wanted.

Off with the old, on with the new. Poor Catherine, but it wasn't going to be poor Sophy.

She said, 'Of course not. Catherine's David's friend, isn't she? She wouldn't be here unless David was. Anyhow, it's none of my business. As I keep telling you, I'm not available.'

'That's your final word?'

He wasn't convinced. He knew that when he touched her her skin sang, and he believed he could hold her as long as he desired her. But she would make him set her free.

She sat hunched, knees under her chin, hands clasped across her ankles, her eyes hooded and cool. 'I don't like men who think they have a God-given right to make the rules,' she said. 'Tycoons, even generous tycoons, are not my favourite people.'

Robert wasn't saying anything, and after a moment or two of silence Sophy went on, 'And I do have a favourite person. A man who suits me very well. We suit each other, and we may get married one of these fine days.'

He said then, 'It sounds a passionate affair.'

'I don't want a passionate affair, that's what I'm telling you. I'm sure you'd make a wonderful lover—you have the experience, haven't you? But if you were my lover you'd be taking second place to another man, and I don't think you'd enjoy that.'

He stood up, tall, broad-shouldered, powerful. 'No,' he said, 'I wouldn't enjoy that,' and she felt his rejection of her as though he had ordered her out of his house.

'I'm glad you're feeling better,' he said formally, as anyone would say whether they meant it or not, and he went, leaving Puppy behind, and she knew she wouldn't see him again, except by accident.

His pride and his arrogance would never stand for what she had just told him. She need not worry about Robert Carlton any more, and she sank back on the pillows, feeling as weak and as ill as though she had cut her wrists and was slowly bleeding to death.

CHAPTER EIGHT

LAST night she had slept soundly, only aware of her surroundings when Catherine Gordon stood beside her bed. But tonight she tossed and turned, slept fitfully and woke feeling drained.

She lay for a little while, remembering how easy it had been in the end to break with Robert Carlton. His arrogance wouldn't let him accept that a woman he wanted might prefer another man. He would simply stop wanting her, because she had shown such appalling taste.

'Let me go,' she had said, and he had, and now she had to go home.

Her clothes were hanging in the wardrobe, the working clothes she had come up here in, jeans and shirt, and her cloak. She went into the little lilac-coloured bathroom that led off the bedroom, and splashed water into her eyes. Then she dressed slowly, her limbs were heavy, and packed the nightdress and accessories Beryl had brought yesterday back into the little case.

Miss Harris had taken Puppy with her last night, when she brought in Sophy's supper. If it hadn't been for collecting him Sophy would have considered leaving a note. 'Dear All, Thank you very much, you couldn't have been kinder, but I simply must not impose on you any longer.' Something like that.

She would have liked to make a quiet and cowardly getaway, but she had to take Puppy with her, so she couldn't pin a note to her pillow—even if she could have found something to write a note with—and try to steal out of the house.

She fastened her cloak and picked up the case and opened the door, stepping on to a landing, passing a beautiful tall grandfather clock, walls lined with pictures, a long dark table and chairs in gleaming old wood.

She would have liked to linger and stare and touch, but there was no time for that, and she was glad to find herself at the top of the main staircase. She could easily have taken a wrong turn, this was quite a large house.

It was just eight o'clock. That was what her watch said, and the grandfather clock confirmed it, striking eight followed by a pure and musical peal of chimes. She was half way down the staircase when Mrs Tewson came into the hall and spotted her.

Sophy steadied herself against the handrail. 'Good morning,' that sounded nice and bright and normal. 'I'm feeling so much better, and I'm going home now, I've caused you all enough trouble.'

Mrs Tewson whisked away down the corridor and Sophy continued down the stairs. At this time on a Sunday morning Robert might not be awake, and Sophy could imagine her knocking on his bedroom door to tell him Sophy was up and off. He wouldn't thank her for bothering him with that news.

The progress she was making wasn't bad. At the bottom of the stairs she leaned against the shining mahogany post and debated whether to call Puppy, who was probably in the kitchen.

If he came rushing into the hall there were all those priceless things he could scatter, so perhaps she had better fetch him; but just then Mrs Tewson came hurrying down the passage with Robert behind her.

He was fully dressed, shaved, and it was Mrs Tewson who was flustered, not him. Mrs Tewson was saying, 'She shouldn't be downstairs, not for two or three days, the doctor said,' talking to him as though Sophy was deaf.

'How do you feel?' asked Robert.

'Much better, thank you,' said Sophy firmly.

'And you want to go home?'

'Oh yes, please.' Of course she wanted to go home.

'Very well,' he said. 'Wait here and I'll bring the car round.'

He smiled at her, and her crazy heart did a slow lurch, although it was a smile he would have given any departing guest.

She sat on the bottom step to wait and Mrs Tewson peered at her and said, 'Your temperature's down, that's something. Now are you sure you're going to be all right?'

'Quite sure,' said Sophy, 'and thank you very much.'

When the front door opened and Robert came in she said, 'There's Puppy.'

'He's in the car.' He picked up the case. He was packing her off without any argument, but she would hardly be convalescing at his expense after their talk last night. She couldn't take without giving, and she wasn't prepared to pay the only price he wanted.

He didn't need to help her walk, she was managing, but he stood near as though she might stumble; and she took good care she did not, walking out on to the forecourt where the car was parked, near to the door.

Puppy sat in the back seat, and wagged his tail and grinned a welcome. 'We both thank you for your hospitality,' she said to Robert, who said nothing.

A few minutes later they drew up in front of The Potter's Wheel, and as Sophy opened her front door she said, 'Goodbye then,' but Robert followed her in, carrying her case.

'Get into bed,' he ordered.

'That's what I'm going to do.'

The living room struck chill, but it was tidy. Either Beryl or Jenine had finished washing up and put things away. There was a fire laid in the grate, and Robert went into the kitchen to fetch the matches, and touched the paper here and there.

'If I'm going to bed,' Sophy might have said, 'I won't be needing that.' But she might get up again later, and it was cheerful to see the wood catching and crackling.

'Off with you,' he said.

'In my own time.' She stayed exactly where she was.

He was watching the fire, his back to her. He said, 'You're under doctor's orders, not mine. I'm not as power-mad as you imagine, I've no wish to influence you.'

He turned, as always it seemed towering over her, and she remembered the warm secret smell of his skin when her face was against his bare chest, the hairs tickling her lips. 'Except,' he said, 'that I would have liked to make love to you. I'm sorry I never overruled you there, I think we might both have found it a rewarding experience.'

Sophy remembered the kiss, and wondered how she would ever stop remembering.

'Is it the man I saw you with in Franco's?' he asked. 'Or the actor who was your very good friend before you came here?'

'Stewart?' Audrey must have told him about Stewart, and that was a shaker, Audrey was usually circumspect in what she said about anyone.

'Stewart Baines,' said Robert. 'Is he a good actor? I don't believe I've ever seen him.'

'Not Stewart,' she gulped. 'I finished with Stewart when I left London.'

'The local man.' He nodded. 'Good! What's his number?'

'What for?'

'You'll need someone to look in on you today.'

'I can phone him myself.' She couldn't summon Giles over to act as nurse. She only hoped he hadn't caught the bug from her last Wednesday, she had been feeling ill then. 'I hope he's all right,' she said.

'Why shouldn't he be?'

'He's the only one I've kissed lately.'

'That could be his misfortune,' said Robert gravely. 'In the meantime I'll ring Mrs Manders.'

She wouldn't mind Beryl coming over. It was too early to be bothering her, but Robert seemed determined to delegate her to somebody before he left and she needed to get to bed. She was still shaky.

'All right,' she said. 'Good morning.'

'Goodbye.' Robert smiled as he said that, but it was final. He didn't have to say, 'I'll never come to your door again or speak to you on the phone. I'll never speak to you at all except as neighbours if we meet, and soon I'll have forgotten how your lips tasted, that I wanted to touch you, to love you...'

He said, 'Goodbye,' and that was the finish of it all. As Sophy went upstairs she heard the phone ping as he started to dial Beryl's number. She got into bed with her clothes on, and her cloak on top of the bedclothes, because the sheets were cold and she was shivering.

Beryl came right round, calling, 'Sophy!' from the bottom of the stairs.

'Hi!' Sophy tried to sound breezy, but her voice lacked conviction. It was a hollow 'Hi!'

She heard Beryl's footsteps clattering on the bare

boards of the staircase—some day she'd buy a stair carpet—and then Beryl was in the room, glaring almost accusingly, demanding, 'What are you doing here?'

'I live here,' said Sophy inanely.

'Are you better?'

'Well, nearly. I'll probably stop in bed today, but I'm nearly back to normal. It's nice to see you, but you shouldn't have dashed round.'

'That's all right.' Beryl was wearing a pinafore under her coat and Sophy asked,

'Were you getting breakfast?'

'No, I was getting myself a cup of tea. I put Stevie in bed with Jim and left them.' Beryl grinned, 'They say there's no place like home, but I liked the bedroom you had yesterday better than this.'

'And there's a carpet on those stairs,' said Sophy.

'So what are you doing back here, this early on a Sunday morning?'

'Oh, I woke up and looked round and wondered what I was doing in some man's house.'

Beryl's grin widened. 'That's what everybody round here would like to know,' she said.

People Sophy didn't know were gossiping about her, because her name had become linked with Robert Carlton. She said, 'They'd best make the best of it, because there isn't going to be any more scandal. He's gone right off me, and he never was my type.' She didn't say that she would probably lie awake tonight yearning for him, aching. 'Too bossy,' she added.

'But he is the boss, isn't he?' Beryl always was practical. 'I mean, all those factories. He could have advised you here, on the business side.'

When Sophy said, 'I don't need his help,' Beryl's eloquent glance swept the bed and Sophy in it. 'Like you said yesterday,' said Sophy, 'I know now.'

Beryl brought her up a hot water bottle, and un-packed the suitcase for Sophy's nightdress and the pills the doctor had left. Before she went she made a pot of tea and boiled an egg, and announced that she would be bringing dinner round between two plates later, and something for Puppy who would be walked, either by Beryl or Jenine or Jim, this evening.

It was Jenine who came to walk Puppy, and by then Sophy was in the living room, still in her dressing gown but pottering around.

Jenine's company was hardly a tonic. The virus was leaving Sophy depressed, but Jenine was doing noth-ing to help, asking over and over why Sophy hadn't *said* how she felt, instead of waiting for Robert Carl-ton to come and then telling him.

Jenine had thought she was Sophy's friend and Sophy should know that Jenine would have called in the doctor, or called in Beryl. If it was Beryl Sophy preferred, said with a sniff.

'It just happened that way,' Sophy kept explaining.

'And what about Giles?' Jenine sounded very cross. 'Does he know Robert Carlton marched in and took you off?'

Jenine's voice was whining between Sophy's ears like a low-pitched buzz saw, and Sophy said wearily, 'No, he doesn't, but if it will make you any happier I'll tell him all about it tomorrow.'

'I'm sure it's none of my business,' said Jenine, get-ting up from her chair. 'I only looked in to walk the dog and cheer you up,' and that made Sophy smile, especially as Jenine was going.

She would phone Giles some time, mainly to check that he was all right, and before she went back to bed she phoned Audrey.

She told her tale of misfortune, the spoiled batch of pots, the virus, but that everyone had been marvellous, and could Audrey get her two silk squares, real silk, and post them here? She described Mrs Tewson and Miss Harris, so that Audrey would have some idea what colours and patterns to choose, and explained who they were, and Audrey thought it was most considerate of Robert to take Sophy home to be nursed by his staff.

'Oh, it was,' said Sophy. 'But we've decided we don't have much in common after all. By the way, what did you tell him about Stewart?'

'*Nothing!*' Audrey was aghast. 'Except that Stewart stopped you taking a partnership. You haven't quarrelled over Stewart?'

'We haven't quarrelled,' Sophy tried to soothe her. 'But didn't it dawn on you that Robert was like Stewart only more so?'

'Not a bit,' said Audrey decisively. 'Well, there might be some resemblance in looks, but Robert is much more assured and mature and——'

'Successful and powerful,' said Sophy. 'And Stewart shoved me around, so what do you think Robert would do?'

Audrey said softly, 'Oh, we *liked* Robert. I always knew that Stewart was selfish, but Robert is masterful.'

'Two words for the same thing,' said Sophy. 'I didn't come up here to jump out of the frying pan into the fire.'

'What about Giles, then?' said Audrey, as though he'd be a very poor consolation prize.

'I saw him on Wednesday. I'm hoping he hasn't caught my 'flu or whatever it is.'

'Robert hasn't?'

'Robert,' said Sophy tartly, 'is strong as a bull.' By

no stretch of imagination could she see him ill or weak. He had wanted her. That was a need, but not a weakness when he could control it like any other appetite that could be satisfied elsewhere.

She said, 'I'll have to ring off, I'm going back to bed now.' She was feeling more and more depressed, because she wasn't strong yet, the virus still lingered. It had nothing to do with wondering who Robert would take in her place.

Sophy's recovery was sure and steady. Each day she felt stronger and by the end of the week she was as fit as she had ever been. But her spirits were taking longer to revive.

Gloom was foreign to her nature, but all this week she had to make an effort to smile. She was working again, sensibly now, eating her meals, organising herself, and setting no over-ambitious deadlines.

Robert returned her order books, Mrs Tewson brought them down on Monday, and on Monday Beryl arrived for work as well as Jenine. She said she had been given three weeks' paid leave, last week, by Mr Carlton, to be in The Potter's Wheel, and she was taking it.

Jenine wasn't too pleased. She was fond of her sister, but she felt that Beryl was invading her territory, even though she didn't want to make pots herself. She stayed in the shop most of the time, looking ethereal and rather glamorous, and eyeing Beryl and Sophy in their working gear, as though they were peasants coming in from the fields.

Sophy missed her Wednesday date with Giles. He rang her on Tuesday. She had been going to ring him, and she asked as soon as she recognised his voice, 'Are you all right?'

He said he was. He'd been busy. Trade was quite good and her pots were selling, and she said, 'That's a relief.'

'Didn't you expect them to sell?'

'I mean that you're well. I've been down with one of those odd bugs and I was worried you might have caught it.'

Round here Sophy seemed to have been the only victim, as though it was her personal private virus, and she was glad she hadn't proved contagious.

Giles said he was sorry and how was she now?

'Not up to coming out, I'm afraid. Nor really to seeing anybody.' She had been in the workroom that day, but talking to Giles made her realise she would be a drag in company, so they left it at next Wednesday perhaps, and Giles sounded sympathetic. He promised to phone again, and said he could get over in the evening any time she wanted to see him.

She didn't particularly want to see him until she felt brighter, but that week she phoned and wrote to some of her old friends. She invited them over, and all the ones she phoned seemed pleased to hear from her and keen to come and see her.

She would buy put-up beds or go to auctions. She would furnish that empty second bedroom as a guest room and have friends to visit. Her life was here now, and she had to fill it if she wasn't going to be lonely.

The week after next she was going along to a birthday party in Halebridge, with Beryl and Jim and Jenine, to meet some young people of her own age. The future was bright, but she was still having these fits of depression.

In the evenings she had to make herself do chores or write letters, or take Puppy for his walk, or she would just have sat there, feeling tired and dull and not at all sure she had made the right decision in coming here.

Perhaps she should have stayed where she was, working for Audrey and her partner. Things were always moving there, there was always somewhere to go, and it was stupid being scared of Stewart.

Stewart, who was shallow and selfish, and only a moderately good actor. She even knew that now, and there were times when she would have liked to turn back the clock.

Except that she would hate to lose Puppy, and she would miss Beryl and even Jenine; and this dissatisfaction was all tied up with letting herself get rundown. Soon she would be happy and contented again, and all her zest for living would come back.

Her first outing was on Friday, when she delivered the first Halebridge Pottery to the post office. The couple who were her customers arranged it while she watched, on a central shelf in the pottery section, with a card 'Halebridge Ware' painted in a bold black flowering script over a grey wash watercolour of the Stones.

Sophy was very taken by the card, and they were delighted with the pottery, so that the transaction concluded in mutual admiration. They were a youngish pair, and could well turn into friends, and she felt better for talking to them. Encouraged in her efforts, and glowing with professional pride.

Puppy was waiting in the car which she had parked in a side street. It was market day today and there was no parking space in the square. Sophy put on his lead and walked around the small town, looking in shop windows, enjoying the sunshine. The last time she had come here she had hurried away, because this was

Robert's town and she had been nervous that she might meet him.

Now it wouldn't matter. It wouldn't happen, he'd hardly be strolling around this time of day, and if she did meet him he was no longer any danger. He wasn't pursuing her any longer. She went up to the Stones each night with Puppy and she had never seen him, so the spell was broken.

At the beginning it was weird, the way their paths crossed. Of course, except for exercising Puppy, this was the first time she had left the house since Robert walked out of it on Monday, but once she would have expected him to turn that corner and stand facing her. Once he had seemed to be everywhere. Well, thank goodness she was free of him these days.

She did a little shopping. She bought some paperbacks, and a new green eyeshadow. She made a hairdressing appointment for next Thursday morning, in a super-looking little salon, and then as it was lunchtime she decided to have lunch.

Robert was unlikely to be in Franco's midday, and it was the only place she knew, and the best place for miles. So she went to Franco's, and had a spaghetti dish with a fabulous sauce, followed by baked peaches stuffed with crushed macaroons.

She ate slowly. After all, she had just concluded a business deal that, with any luck, should go on and on. Why shouldn't she treat herself to a good meal and take her time over it? She sipped her coffee while the tables around her emptied, and looked at her watch and knew that no one else was likely to come in for lunch now. Then she left.

Of course she wasn't disappointed. She hadn't gone in there for anything but the food, and the food had been well worth the money.

Next morning the silk squares she had asked Audrey to buy for her arrived. Blue for Mrs Tewson, navy and turquoise in a geometric pattern; and swirling pink and beige for Miss Harris. They were pure silk, soft enough to crush into a tiny ball and then fall free without a crease. Sophy hoped they'd like them. She'd take them up this evening.

She also had a letter from a girl she had worked with in the solicitor's office—one she had written to on Monday—who said she'd like to come down to Hale-bridge. She could get a couple of days tacked on a weekend more or less any time. The staff who had been there in Sophy's day sent their love, and were tickled to hear she now had her own pottery and was launching her own brand.

'Mr Lowndes,' the senior partner, her father's friend, 'says your father would have been proud of you. He would, wouldn't he? He was a great guy, your father. We could do with a few more like him around these days.'

'Not bad news?' asked Beryl anxiously, seeing her expression, and Sophy shook her head.

'No. From someone where I used to live. I was just thinking about my father. He was—well, he wasn't easy to get on with. He never seemed to understand, and I suppose I never understood him either.'

'Nothing for me, of course,' said Jenine, who had been serving when the post arrived.

'No,' said Beryl, and Jenine shrugged. She wasn't rushing for the mail any longer, as though she had stopped expecting David to write.

Sophy was alone in the shop that afternoon. Saturday had always been half-day for Jenine, and Beryl was working the same hours as Jenine. Nothing much happened, few customers came in and the only phone call was from Giles.

Sophy invited him to tea tomorrow. It was either that or he was coming over tonight, and she really couldn't stand him tonight. She said, 'Jenine asked to be remembered to you,' for something to say, and Jenine had, earlier in the week. 'Remember me to Giles when you ring him,' Jenine had said.

'Oh yes?' Giles was obviously flattered. 'A nice girl, very pretty.'

'Isn't she?' said Sophy, and thought she might go round in the morning and ask Jenine to tea too. They could suit each other, both looking for a marriage partner. Anyhow, they could talk to each other. Sophy didn't feel she was going to be sparkling company herself. It had been a humid week, although the sun had shone. She wondered if the weather had had anything to do with her depression.

When she closed the shop she decided to take up the scarves before she got tea. Perhaps climbing the hill would blow away the cobwebs, although there wasn't a breeze. It was warm and still when she walked past the Stones, through the little wood, and round to the front door.

Miss Harris answered and Sophy handed over her gifts and thanked them again, and said that any time they were free please would they come and have tea with her?

'Won't you come in?' invited Miss Harris.

Sophy hesitated. 'I don't think so. I've got him with me.' That was Puppy, although he'd had the freedom of this house before. 'And I'm sure you're busy.'

'We are expecting company,' Miss Harris admitted, 'but I know Mrs Tewson——'

'Some other time, then,' said Sophy, and went, smiling and quickly. She would hate to get cornered in here when the company arrived, whoever the company was. She had to get home and have her tea, and write a few letters. That was what she had to do.

When she got home she went to her bureau and put this morning's letter into one of the cubbyholes, and opened the drawer into which she had dropped the airmails Robert had sent her. She read them again, one after the other.

They weren't love letters. People kept love letters. These were here because it was only a few days since they'd arrived and she hadn't got round to clearing them out. She was reading them this once and then she would tear them up.

When she had finished she made a pile of them.

No one had ever sent her love letters. When she had lived in her father's home boys who liked her lived in the same town and phoned her, at work usually. Then there had been Stewart, who saw her almost every day.

She had never written a love letter nor received one, and she remembered a bundle of letters she had found in her father's desk. She was clearing up, selling up, and they were from her mother to her father, written before they married. She had only read a little, it had seemed an intrusion, like spying on strangers.

She had burned them with all the other papers. They must have been there a long time. He must have put them there years before, and forgotten them she had thought then; but she remembered now how they had looked, in their tidy pile fastened together with a thin blue ribbon, a little creased, the edges tattered.

She knew now that he had read them again and again, because they were the voice of the woman he loved. That he had kept them because he loved her and there was no other woman he would ever want.

Just as she would keep these letters—and she looked down at them in something approaching horror.

I love him, she thought; oh, my God, I love him; and what can I do about that that won't finish me in the end?

It made sense of her depression. She knew now why she had hung about Halebridge, gone into Franco's, walked up to the Stones each night and to the house just now. She had been looking for Robert because the sight of him would have made her happy.

It had never been like this with Stewart. That had always been on the surface, but this feeling of longing and loss permeated her whole being. 'I don't like tycoons,' she had said, 'even kind ones.' Well, she liked Robert. Without him the days seemed hardly worth the effort, and the nights were going to get worse.

The nights had been bleak enough this week, but they could get worse, and her mind shrank from considering such a future.

She had to see him. Of course he didn't feel the same way about her, but he might be pleased to see her, and she had to see him, and talk to him.

She'd talk business: Halebridge ware in the post office and Beryl proving an apt pupil. She'd thank Robert once more for putting her in one of his guest rooms and calling the doctor. She was fine again now, she'd say, healthy as could be.

Oh, and if he remembered what she had said about Giles—well, that was off, it was never really on, and she hoped they could be friends again, she and Robert.

She certainly hoped they could be friends, because whatever happened to her with him couldn't be as cold and destroying as what would happen to her without him.

She couldn't tell him that, but now she had admitted it to herself she would find a way to see him again. She might phone him. She wished now that she had gone in to speak to Mrs Tewson, she would probably have seen Robert then, she might have been asked to stay a while, even if there was company, even if the company did include Catherine Gordon.

She watched television after tea, without really seeing it, and when the usual time for Puppy's walk came round Puppy became restless, whining at the door, rolling beseeching eyes at Sophy.

'You've been up the hill once tonight,' she pointed out, but she wasn't strongly averse to going again. It was better than sitting here, staring at flickering images when her thoughts wouldn't let her concentrate on what they were saying.

'You're a trier,' she said, letting him out of the kitchen door, adding wryly, 'You and me both, but your wants are easier met.'

He was off, through the fence and up the hill, and she followed him over the familiar track. The heaviness of the day was a pleasant mildness now. Moon and stars were out and all was quiet when she reached the Stones.

The windows of the house might be open on such a warm night, but no sound reached her through the little wood. She had wondered if she might hear music.

The company might be a party for all she knew, although she felt that if it was it would be a dinner party. She could visualise Robert presiding over a dinner table with wit and charm, rather than filling his home with jostling guests eating canapés and balancing glasses.

It could be a business meeting, of course, or something intimate, like dinner for two. She could imagine a dinner for two and a girl looking like Catherine Gordon, even if she wasn't Catherine Gordon, and pain shot through her so that her very breath hurt.

Puppy had moved into the trees, he usually did that since they had stayed at the house. Probably the memory of food called him, and Sophy always said, 'Don't you go away.'

She said it now, 'Puppy, don't go away,' standing in the horseshoe of the great standing stones, asking them idiotically, 'Any of you a wishing stone?'

Perhaps she could stroll along to the house and pretend that Puppy had run on ahead, he wouldn't need any encouragement to do that. She could ask to see Robert, she could say it was about Beryl.

He was paying Beryl for these three weeks at The Potter's Wheel before she went back to the factory and part-time for Sophy, and that was hardly fair. She could say she felt she ought to be paying something.

At least she'd see Robert, and she'd know if the company was only one, and if it was she could come away and cry.

She pressed her face against a Stone. Some archaeologists said these old standing stones gave out a strange heat, and this one wasn't cold. But the night wasn't cold, only her heart was, and she wished for Robert. She wished for him with all her strength, and she heard Puppy coming panting back and Robert said, 'What was the wish?'

She stood there gasping, she couldn't have been more astounded if he had appeared in a puff of smoke, and when he held out his arms she ran into them as though they were meeting again after a long time.

It was like the hug of friends at an airport, comforting and reassuring, and for the moment it was enough to be this close again. 'What was the wish?' he asked again. 'We might be able to do something about it.'

He had heard her asking them, 'Are you a wishing stone?' and although he might suspect he might have featured, she could easily be wishing for something or somebody else.

But he was kind, he would help her if he could, and how could she help loving him?

She said, 'It worked. I wanted to see you. To say hello, and tell you I'm fighting fit again.'

She had been fit enough a moment ago, but now her leg were shaking. She mustn't cling to him, that kind of weakness might embarrass him, it would certainly embarrass her. She added, 'I was told you had company.'

'I have, but I'm taking a walk.'

It wasn't dinner for two, or he wouldn't be walking alone. There must be enough of them to entertain themselves. With an arm still around her he looked out across the Downs. 'Come with me?' he said.

'Yes.'

He knew the Downs. They wouldn't get lost, unfortunately, and it wouldn't rain, it was a lovely night.

They went down the hill, away from the Stones, by the path, and this time the ground was dry, and followed a path covered with bracken instead of the squelchy moss she had plodded through before.

They talked about Beryl, what a help she was going to be. Sophy told him about having delivered her Halebridge ware and he said he was sure it would sell well, he'd like to see it. He would, she assured him.

'Mrs Tewson and Miss Harris are very pleased with the scarves,' he told her.

'It was little enough, they were very kind. Audrey got them for me. You met Audrey?'

'I did,' he said.

She had thought that the Downs in the dark would be frightening, but tonight they were warm and the moonlight was just light enough. They walked for ten minutes or so, then Robert took off his coat and put it down for her to sit on, and sat down himself, looking at her.

At last he asked, 'How's Giles?'

'He didn't catch my bug.' Puppy was circling them, within the ring of moonlight, busily snuffling but going nowhere until they did. 'He's coming to tea tomorrow,' said Sophy. 'I'm asking Jenine too. I think they should get on well together.'

'Excellent idea.' His voice was warm and smiling and she wanted to creep into his arms. She picked a blade of grass and nibbled on it and said,

'I thought the spell had broken. The affinity.'

'No.' It was good to know that. It made the future safe.

Sophy was so glad that she felt happiness must be bursting out of her in golden rays. 'It was uncanny at first, wasn't it?' she said, 'the way we met everywhere. But nowhere this week, although I came up here every night. I even went into Franco's for lunch yesterday, hoping I might see you.'

She didn't mind telling him that and he chuckled. 'When you first came here I asked Mrs Tewson what she knew about you and she went down to the pottery, presumably to get a look at you, and told me you were going to Franco's that night. That's why I was there.'

'*Really?*' Her laughter was soft, delighted. It was much better to know that he had engineered their meetings. He asked,

'Are you going to overlook me being a tycoon? I don't much care for the description.'

'I'll try.' Suddenly she was admitting, 'I've been

prejudiced and pig-headed, but you see Stewart had to be boss, and knowing Stewart didn't do me much good. And before Stewart my father ordered my life about it, and I resented it, and I'm only just beginning to realise that he loved me, but I was always the child to him that my mother had left in his care, and he only wanted to protect me.'

'And you don't want to be protected?'

She did, by him. When she was feeling ill and he came she had simply given up, and known she would be safe. If he hadn't come she would have battled on, but when he was near her deepest instincts were to lean on him.

She dropped the blade of grass and picked another with some care, looking at it as though it might be a rare specimen. 'Sometimes, with you,' she said. 'You weaken me. When I'm with you I want to give in, and then I've been scared you'd make all the rules— because you do make the rules, don't you?'

She felt his hands on her, jerking her round, and his voice was harsh. 'Tell me something,' he said, 'how the hell could I rule you when you could break me?'

'That's crazy.'

He held her, facing him, speaking slowly as though she must hear and believe each word. 'I've waited up there every night to see you walk round the Stones, because you're inside me, I couldn't tear you out without killing myself. Until I met you there was never anyone I wanted to be near for the rest of my life. Without you I am broken.'

He was the strongest man she had ever met, but now she reached for him and held him tenderly. With no one else would he lose control of himself in the smallest way, but with her he was without defences. They were one person, two halves of one person, only complete and whole together.

She kissed his face with quick delicate kisses as a child might, but she was a woman with her man and soon the kisses would change. He would kiss her, taking what she was aching to give, and she could feel her heart beating hard beneath his hand. She said, 'All week I've been writing to my friends, inviting them over, I thought I was going to have a lot of time on my own.'

'There's room for them,' he said.

'Where?'

'In our home.'

'Am I moving in?'

'Where would my wife be living, except with me?'

His breath had been warm on her lips, but he wasn't breathing now. He was waiting for what she would say, and of course she would marry him.

It wasn't like Jenine and Giles, who were both looking desperately for a partner. Sophy hadn't been searching and neither had Robert, but they had come together so surely that nothing in this world would ever part them.

'Of course,' she said, and he said,

'Thank God for that.' Then he smiled, 'We'll go back in a while and tell them.'

'Who are they?' If she had known she was going to be introduced to Robert's guests as his future wife she would have tidied herself up a little before she came out, but how could she have imagined that anything so wonderful might happen?

He said, 'Old friends, you'll like them; and they'll certainly like you.'

'Catherine Gordon?'

'No.'

'Was she David's friend?'

'One of David's friends.'

'But she preferred you?'

'Yes.'

'I don't blame her.' Her smile was slanting, mischievous. 'I prefer you myself.'

'I hope so.' He knew she had been jealous, and she knew that he had suffered when she had told him she preferred Giles, but now it was a smiling matter.

She said, 'I thought you'd given me up when I told you about Giles.'

'Now that *is* crazy, I don't have any pride where you're concerned. He looked down at her, where she lay back on the bracken, her hair loose, her eyes dark and wide. He said huskily, 'My sweet stubborn love, you're the witch of the Stones, do you know that? Like the eighth man, if I had to I'd follow you as long as I live.'

His shoulders blocked out the stars, and she looked up into his face with its hard mouth and strong jaw, and knew the passion and the tenderness he felt for her, and whispered, 'What do you think happened when he caught the witch?'

He laughed softly. 'I hope she decided she didn't want to turn him into stone, that she preferred him as flesh and blood.'

She laughed too, and as his mouth came down on hers she managed to say, 'Yes, oh *yes* ...'

Harlequin

COLLECTION
EDITIONS OF 1978

Harlequin's Collection 1?

ANDREA BLAKE
**Night of
the Hurrica**

Harlequin's Collection 106   1.25

ANNE WEALE
**If This
Is Love**

**50 great stories
of special beauty
and significance**

$1.25
each novel

In 1976 we introduced the first 100 Harlequin Collections—a selection of titles chosen from our best sellers of the past 20 years. This series, a trip down memory lane, proved how great romantic fiction can be timeless and appealing from generation to generation. The theme of love and romance is eternal, and, when placed in the hands of talented, creative, authors whose true gift lies in their ability to write from the heart, the stories reach a special level of brilliance that the passage of time cannot dim. Like a treasured heirloom, an antique of superb craftsmanship, a beautiful gift from someone loved—these stories too, have a special significance that transcends the ordinary. **$1.25 each novel**

Here are your 1978
Harlequin Collection Editions...

Original Harlequin Romance numbers in brackets

ORDER FORM
Harlequin Reader Service

In U.S.A.
MPO Box 707
Niagara Falls, N.Y. 14302

In Canada
649 Ontario St.,
Stratford, Ontario, N5A 6W2

Please send me the following Harlequin Collection novels. I am enclosing my check or money order for $1.25 for each novel ordered, plus 25¢ to cover postage and handling.

☐ 102	☐ 115	☐ 128	☐ 140
☐ 103	☐ 116	☐ 129	☐ 141
☐ 104	☐ 117	☐ 130	☐ 142
☐ 105	☐ 118	☐ 131	☐ 143
☐ 106	☐ 119	☐ 132	☐ 144
☐ 107	☐ 120	☐ 133	☐ 145
☐ 108	☐ 121	☐ 134	☐ 146
☐ 109	☐ 122	☐ 135	☐ 147
☐ 110	☐ 123	☐ 136	☐ 148
☐ 111	☐ 124	☐ 137	☐ 149
☐ 112	☐ 125	☐ 138	☐ 150
☐ 113	☐ 126	☐ 139	☐ 151
☐ 114	☐ 127		

Number of novels checked @
$1.25 each = $ _____
N.Y. and N.J. residents add
appropriate sales tax $ _____
Postage and handling $ ___.25_

TOTAL $ _____

NAME _____
_____(Please Print)_____
ADDRESS _____
CITY _____
STATE/PROV. _____
ZIP/POSTAL CODE _____

AB ROM 2217